Prime Shot

Patricia Fisher Ship's Detective Book 10

Steve Higgs

Text Copyright © 2025 Steven J Higgs

Publisher: Steve Higgs

The right of Steve Higgs to be identified as author of the Work has been asserted by him in accordance with the Copyright, Designs and Patents Act 1988

All rights reserved.

The book is copyright material and must not be copied, reproduced, transferred, distributed, leased, licensed or publicly performed or used in any way except as specifically permitted in writing by the publishers, as allowed under the terms and conditions under which it was purchased or as strictly permitted by applicable copyright law. Any unauthorised distribution or use of this text may be a direct infringement of the author's and publisher's rights and those responsible may be liable in law accordingly.

'Prime Shot' is a work of fiction. Names, characters, businesses, organisations, places, events and incidents either are the product of the author's imagination or are used fictitiously. Any resemblance to actual persons, living or dead, events or locations is entirely coincidental.

Contents

1. Crumbs — 1
2. Blood on the Deck — 5
3. Jewellery Heist — 9
4. Political Minefield — 13
5. Friends — 21
6. Mystery Guest — 28
7. Concealed — 32
8. Sisterhood — 35
9. A Friend in Need — 40
10. Politician Through and Through — 44
11. An Old Friend Comes to Stay — 51
12. My Team — 55
13. Address the Ship — 63
14. Master Criminal — 67
15. Sandwich — 70

16.	Attempted Murder	74
17.	Description	82
18.	Bounty Hunters	87
19.	Body Guarding is Tough	91
20.	Pool of Suspects	95
21.	Unwelcome News	99
22.	Wife Beater	101
23.	Search the Ship!	106
24.	Losing My Cool	112
25.	Public Enemy Number One	116
26.	Breakfast Chatter	121
27.	First Name Terms	128
28.	Missing Something	135
29.	Team Meeting	140
30.	Skill Set	146
31.	Closing the Net	151
32.	Time to Die	159
33.	Airtag	166
34.	Cocktail Party	172
35.	The Real Target	178
36.	The Truth of It	181
37.	Itchy Skull	185
38.	Morris Bail Bonds	191
39.	Barbie's Research	196

40. Sickbay	199
41. Good Shot	204
42. Staged?	207
43. Really Badly Wrong	212
44. Ambush	215
45. Slightly Deranged	221
46. Finding Dale	224
47. Bedlam	230
48. Shot in the Back	236
49. The Press Conference	240
50. Dinner	250
51. Heist	254
52. Author's Notes:	256
53. What's next for Patricia Fisher?	259
54. Did you Miss Patricia's Adventure in Australia?	261
55. Free Books and More	263

Crumbs

I held the crouch and ignored the smell of cleaning fluids. There were crumbs on the floor next to what appeared to be a makeshift seat/bed.

"Has this happened before?" I posed the question without looking around to see the person standing behind me.

"No, Mrs Fisher."

I was on deck eight where one of the cleaning crews – there is one for every deck – had reported a robbery from their storeroom. Two of the cleaners, Carl and Marisol had returned to fetch their lunches only to find them missing. Or, more accurately, to find someone had eaten them. The perpetrator left behind an apple core, the twiggy bit from which they had plucked Marisol's grapes, the wrapper from a chocolate bar, and the wrappers from both their sandwiches.

Marisol had gone to the restroom, leaving me with Carl.

My name is Patricia Fisher and I work on a cruise ship as a detective. The ship has lots of security officers to keep the passengers safe and make sure no one who shouldn't be getting on board can do so. They make sure weapons stay on the shore and perform many other tasks, but crime happens much the same as anywhere else on the planet, and that's where I come in.

I tried to rise out of my crouch in an elegant manner that would show off my core strength and muscular control. When my legs protested and threatened to give way, I snatched at Carl's trousers.

He tried to dance out of the way which pulled me off balance. Now pitching forward, I clung to his legs only to find he wasn't wearing a belt. He also wasn't wearing any underwear.

The trousers came down, I fell onto my knees, and the door opened.

Framed in the doorway, Marisol's mouth dropped open. I was kneeling on the deck with my face level with Carl's groin. I had his trousers in my hands and a shocked look on my face. The only saving grace was that my mouth was firmly closed.

Carl ripped his trousers out of my hands, yanking them back into place while Marisol very deliberately placed first one hand and then the other on her hips.

"It's not what it looks like," Carl protested. "She fell."

"I fell," I repeated what he said.

Marisol didn't look even slightly convinced. "And look at what you almost landed on."

This is so utterly typical for me. I try to dress nice and act in the manner of a middle-aged English lady, but somehow I always mess it up. I fall over. I walk into things ... I accidentally pull a man's trousers down.

Carl, his face the colour of a beetroot, got some distance between us and I pushed off the deck with my hands to get back to my feet.

"I'm afraid there isn't a lot here for me to investigate," I said, going back to the case as if nothing had happened.

"Mm-hmmm," said Marisol, eyeing me suspiciously. "Well, someone stole my lunch, and we are not the first victims. The team on deck ten got hit yesterday."

"Really?" They hadn't reported it, but then I guess most people wouldn't consider it worth the effort. Truthfully, I was only here now because the last few weeks had been particularly quiet for me.

"Yes," said Marisol. "Just the same as this. Food was taken and it looked as though someone had made a bed out of cardboard boxes and trash bags. I think there is a stowaway."

I doubted that would prove to be the case. Stowaways are rare, but I supposed that I couldn't rule it out entirely.

"Have you thought about locking the storeroom door?"

Marisol laughed. "I doubt anyone has seen a key for that lock in years. Hey, Carl. Have you ever seen a key for the door?"

He shook his head and refused to make eye contact.

Marisol added, "It's the same for the other storerooms so far as I know. There's nothing of any value to lock away and the maintenance teams all have higher priority tasks to worry about. I doubt anyone has even wasted their time asking to have the lock changed in the last year."

I promised that I would continue to investigate and asked that they speak with the other cleaning crews to make sure any further incidents were reported. This wasn't a big crime that would make the papers, but it still fell under my remit to solve.

Leaving the cleaners' storeroom, I headed back up through the ship to get to my suite. It was time to walk the dogs.

Blood on the Deck

Life on board a cruise ship is never the same two days in a row. Nor is it what I believe most people might imagine. By its very nature the scenery is ever changing. Yes, there might be nothing but ocean to look at for several days in a row sometimes, but that is relatively rare and if one tires of its magnificence, there is plenty to distract one's eyes inside the ship.

I, for one, am yet to find the views anything but awe-inspiring, which is why I was paying little attention to what my dogs were doing. We were out for an early evening stroll around the top deck, as is our regular practice, when their insistent tugging pulled my eyes away from the spectacular view.

"Have you found something, girls?"

Anna and Georgie are my pair of miniature dachshunds, although to be factually correct Georgie is a dachshund corgi cross after naughty Anna snuck into Queen Elizabeth's chambers to get frisky with one of her dogs. They go almost everywhere with me and get to be on the cruise ship because I am staying in the royal suite. I can explain more about how that came about later. For now, I was far more interested in what was getting my girls so excited.

Jammed under the edge of a lifeboat mounted at the outside edge of the deck, only their backsides were showing, their little tails sticking out ramrod straight, which told me whatever they had found was supremely distracting. Planting my feet, I hauled them back, fighting their desire to remain in place. They dug their claws in, but they weigh so little I could easily thwart their best efforts to return to whatever it was.

I cooed sweet words and promised a gravy bone when I tied their leads to a rail.

There were other passengers on the deck, but none paying any attention to me or to what I was doing when I got on my knees to peer under the lifeboat. Prepared to be startled when a mouse or rat shot out, I was not expecting to find a small plastic bag. It was the type one uses for food storage with the zip lock top. I couldn't see what was in it, but the zippy bit wasn't fully closed and that had allowed the contents to leak.

I might have wrinkled my nose and walked away, leaving it to be dealt with by someone else, but the leaking liquid was distinctly red. Red like blood, one might say.

"Everything all right down there?" asked a voice from behind me.

The unexpectedness of it made me jump, and I almost bumped my head on the side of the lifeboat.

"Goodness. I'm so sorry," the man apologised. "I didn't mean to startle you. Do you need a hand at all?"

Staying where I was, I said, "One moment, please," and fished a latex glove from my pocket. For speed, I used it as one might an oven glove to pinch one corner of the plastic bag.

"Did you drop something?" the man asked, nosily bending at the waist to get a better look at what I was doing.

With the bag between my fingertips, I pulled it into the light and came out of my crouch. The bag was now on the deck and yet again my dogs were straining to get to it. I could now see why. There was a piece of what appeared to be steak in it. Raw steak. At least I sincerely hoped that was what it was.

"My dogs could smell it," I explained to the man. Wrapping the glove in a tissue, I popped it into my handbag and extended my hand. "Hello, I'm Patricia Fisher."

"Justin Masters," the man introduced himself, clasping my hand in his. He was English, his accent not too dissimilar from mine, though I thought I could detect a Chelsea twang to some of his words. His age had to be close to ninety, which fitted the cruise ship demographic – we get a lot of pensionable age travellers. Dressed in loose-fitting grey trousers, a white shirt and deep red tie, plus a navy blazer buttoned up despite the warm air, he was every bit the well-to-do dapper English gent. He'd also taken an interest in what he'd thought to be a lady in need of a hand, and I warmed to him immediately.

"You're in one of the top deck suites, aren't you?" I enquired, certain I'd seen him following his luggage as porters carried it in that direction when we departed Sydney two days ago.

He smiled broadly. "That's right. A little treat to myself. Can't take it with you," he joked. "You're that sleuth, aren't you?"

It's a good thing I wasn't a spy or someone attempting undercover work because I get recognised all the time. Sleuth is not a word I would employ to describe myself, yet I understand it fits. Purple Star Cruise Lines employs me as a ship's detective, which is to say that like any other microcosm of society, there are crimes committed on the ship and someone needs to catch the perpetrators. I used to be a cleaner and a housewife. My husband earned good money and somewhere along the way I fell into a rut I might never have climbed out of had I not caught him in bed with my best friend.

Long story short, I ran away to sea, got into the kind of trouble that gets a person dead or imprisoned, and in solving my way out of that mess, discovered an ability to unravel mysteries.

Returning Justin's smile with one I hoped was modest and coy, I said, "Yes. That's me. That's why I was fishing around under a lifeboat. I thought … I mean, I could see blood and worried it might be …" The sentence didn't need to be finished, but now that we were both looking down at the bag, I could see there was something else in it besides the steak.

"I say," said Justin. "Isn't that a …"

I dropped back into a crouch, one knee hovering just a fraction of an inch off the deck. Continuing to hope the meat would prove to be bovine (or some other red meat farm animal) I employed the glove once again to prod the contents.

Poking out from under the steak sized piece of meat was something very gold in colour. Very gold because that's precisely what it was. Unable to get the meat to move so I could get a proper look at it, I flipped the bag.

Justin said, "Golly." It echoed what I was thinking, even if I might have chosen a different word to express my surprise.

In the bag with the raw steak was a gold necklace with a ruby the size of my thumb at the centre. Surrounding the gemstone were diamonds, each of them bigger than the one I had in my old engagement ring. I supposed it could be costume jewellery, but I doubted that would be the case. That's just not how things go for me.

Jewellery Heist

The necklace changed how I needed to act. Taking my radio from my handbag, I pressed the send button.

"Patricia for Martin, over." I'm supposed to use ranks and codes and stuff, but radioing for Lieutenant Commander Baker is such a mouthful that I use first names for my team. I suspect there are members of the crew who roll their eyes and mutter about my informality, but I'm dating the captain, so they can just put up with it.

A few seconds was all it took for him to respond.

"Martin here."

I gave him my location and asked that he bring an evidence kit. We were away from the sun lounge that dominates the midships section of the top deck, and toward the bow on the port side. That meant there weren't many passengers about, but there were some, and those who passed all wanted to linger and had to be asked to move along. Weirdly, I felt no need to send Justin on his way. There was no gold band on his ring finger, and he wasn't looking around to check if a companion might be looking to catch up.

We don't get many people travelling alone, but there are always some and I cannot help but worry they feel lonely. He wasn't in my way, and I could see no harm in letting him keep me company for a few minutes.

I was going to strike up a conversation by asking him about his destination, when he surprised me by posing a question about the necklace.

"Do you think perhaps it came from that robbery in Sydney?"

Mystified, I had to ask, "What robbery? Sorry, I must have missed the news."

His eyebrows folded inward for a moment, his brain whirring before he snapped his fingers. "Sorry, I assumed you would have heard about it, given your line of work. Though I suppose it was a little mundane compared with the billions in treasure you found on the San José."

The San José was a recent case that took me forever to solve. Starting with the unidentified body of a stowaway found in the bowels of the ship, the mystery led me around the world and forced me to abandon my post on the Aurelia when a treasure hunter called Xavier Silvestre kidnapped one of my friends. I gave chase with the rest of my team and in getting her back we uncovered the whereabouts of a lost Spanish treasure taken from a ship called the San José more than three hundred years earlier. Finding it landed me squarely back on the front page of the papers around the world.

"Anyway," Justin continued, "there was a heist the night before we left. I guess that's what one might call it. Wallace Bingley's was robbed, the thieves taking an estimated eighteen million dollars' worth of jewellery. It was on the TV news."

I looked at the necklace again, and a dread feeling settled into my gut. I knew of Wallace Bingley's by reputation only. The store catered to the biggest and brightest, to billionaires, oligarchs, and those who could afford to pay the price.

PRIME SHOT

To get in one had to make an appointment and rumour had it most people are simply told no when they apply.

Was I looking at a stolen item from a robbery that happened just a few hours ago? I certainly hoped not because if it was on the ship then it stood to reason to believe the rest of the stolen items were. And the robbers.

That made it my problem.

The sound of running feet brought my head and eyes around to spot Martin coming my way at a jog. By his side was Schneider, the tall, muscular Austrian security officer who insists on going by his last name.

"What have we got?" Martin asked.

"My girls sniffed it out," I explained, drawing their attention to the strange bloody bag. "It was under the edge of the lifeboat, tucked in where they couldn't easily get to it." I stopped talking to ponder how it could have got there. It couldn't have been there long because the steak would have turned nasty very quickly in the heat of the Australian summer.

Now there were four of us around the bag, all staring down at it.

"Why would someone put a steak in a bag with a necklace?" asked Justin.

Martin pulled a face and met my eyes. "Are we sure it's steak?"

I grimaced. "No, but we hope it is."

Schneider got on his belly to look under the lifeboat. "I can see where it was. It was leaking. I'll take a swab and check for prints, but I doubt we will find much down here in the dust under a lifeboat."

I felt sure he was right. Nevertheless, we had to proceed in an appropriate manner.

Martin placed the zip-lock bag and its content in a large evidence bag from his kit.

Anna and Georgie looked most displeased. With the steak now out of their reach, I reclaimed their leads and prepared to resume our walk. I would need to deal with the necklace, but not until after Martin confirmed what creature the meat came from. Praying it would prove to be beef, there remained the mystery of how it came to be in the bag with the piece of jewellery. That was puzzling enough, but secondary to finding a home for the necklace itself.

Schneider jumped back to his feet and dusted down the front of his white uniform with his hands. He and Martin needed a few minutes to look around for other evidence, but I could leave them to it and was just about to ask Justin if he wanted to join me when a scream rang out.

Political Minefield

My feet twitched, but not with indecision. Out on the open water it is often hard to pinpoint which direction a sound came from. Noises bounce off the ship's superstructure, so I waited for the cries of alarm to start.

It took about half a second.

Justin's eyebrows were high on his forehead. "Golly. Did I just hear someone scream?"

There was no time to give him an answer, my legs were already moving. Over one shoulder I called, "Sorry, Justin. I have to go." I slapped the dog leads into Martin's hand. Taking them with me probably wouldn't be sensible, so without looking back, I yelled, "Drop them at my cabin!" and powered down the port side of the deck.

Behind me, I heard Martin whack Schneider on the shoulder and shout, "You go! I've got this."

I'm in my fifties, but fitter than any point since my early twenties thanks to one of my friends who is a gym instructor and a constant bully. I have also learned to wear shoes that allow fast perambulation. Though I would be happier in something elegant with a low heel, Sketchers get the job done and with some wardrobe adjustment can be made to match my outfits well enough.

Of course, even at my fastest Schneider caught me before I could cover twenty yards. He slowed to my pace until I flared my eyes and motioned that he should shift his butt.

There was no good reason why someone would scream in pain on board the ship. No good reason at all. There were, however, lots of bad reasons, and this was going to be one of them.

I covered the hundred or so yards back to the swimming pool and sun lounge area in a little under thirty seconds. By then I was thoroughly out of breath and had a stitch in my right side. Rounding the corner, I slowed to a walk, both to get my breath back and because running into a potentially dangerous and unknown situation is a poor strategy.

In warm climates such as this one, the sun terrace is always busy. Even when the sun goes down you will find people relaxing by and in the pool. The lifeguards close it down and move everyone away at ten o'clock, but right now it was about as busy as it could get.

Toppled sun loungers, tipped over in haste as passengers ran to get away, were strewn in every direction. Not that the people had gone far. No second scream had followed the first and there was no ongoing drama that I could see. People in swimsuits peered out from their hiding places at the edges of the sun terrace. They were under parasols, just inside the doors leading back inside the ship, and peering around the side of the structure. They were also beginning to return now that they could see no reason not to.

To the starboard side of the main pool, next to one of the many cocktail bars, a small crowd had gathered, and I could hear a man ranting in a language I could neither understand nor identify, though it sounded European to my untrained ear.

Ahead of me, Schneider was pushing his way through the crowd of people. As they parted, I saw someone on the deck, and my heart skipped a beat.

An arrow? I only caught a glimpse, but the body lying flat on its back appeared to have an arrow shaft protruding from it. There hadn't been a death on board in the six weeks since I returned to the ship, and I did not need one today.

Thankfully, I was proven overly pessimistic when the passenger in question let out a cry of pain.

At a walking pace, I went around the pool sucking in deep lungfuls of air. I wanted to appear calm and in control when I arrived to take charge. Unfortunately, my slower pace meant others got there before me. And by *others* I mean the captain of the ship.

Alistair Huntley is just the other side of fifty-five and far too handsome to be dating me, in my opinion. Thankfully, he doesn't share my thoughts on the matter, for which I am very grateful. I don't need to be reminded how gorgeous he is, but timing it perfectly to make my heart flutter, he burst through a set of double doors to appear on the deck looking like an action hero coming to save the day.

Half a dozen of the ship's security team tailed him like secret service agents around the US President.

I watched Schneider snap out a crisp salute and because I was paying far too much attention to the captain and his entourage, I walked into a sun lounger. The expletive I spat came out louder than intended to guarantee people would look my way. When Alistair looked up, I was hopping and swearing and pulling a face. It served me right for gawping at my boyfriend.

"We have a wounded passenger, sir," Schneider reported, then levelled his gaze at those around him. "Did anyone see where the arrow came from?"

"Yes," said a short, tubby man in a pair of bright green swim shorts. "He was up there by the helipad, and he was aiming at me. I saw him."

A woman I took to be the man's wife gripped his shoulders as though for support. She looked badly shaken, not that he was paying her any mind.

Alistair delegated Lieutenant Commander Kibble to clear the entire upper deck. There was a person with a bow somewhere and we had passengers in the open. Sending them back to their cabins would keep them out of harm's way and give the security team room to work.

With his team of white-uniformed security officers herding frightened passengers away from the pool, Alistair then sent Schneider with a team of four to check the helipad. I doubted the archer hung around, but if they were fast they might intercept them coming down from the restricted area.

Schneider yelled orders into his radio as they sped away. Through the double doors to my right, paramedics arrived at the scene. They had a fold out gurney and med kit with them – everything they needed to treat in place before moving a patient to the sickbay below decks.

We made space for the paramedics to do their work and dealt with the more pressing issue – the unidentified archer.

"This was an assassination attempt!" the man who claimed he was the target ranted in English. "The security on this ship is terrible. I could have been killed! This isn't just another random attack. Someone tried to throw my country into chaos."

PRIME SHOT

I opened my mouth to speak. I had a whole bunch of questions, but Alistair got there first.

"Prime Minister, I can assure you the security on this ship is first rate. We will get to the bottom of what happened and why as swiftly as possible and the assassin, if this was a deliberate attempt on your life, will be caught."

I searched my brain, trying to place the short, stout man, but I had no clue who he was. Clearly the prime minister of somewhere, he had every right to be shocked.

"Perhaps we should get the prime minister under cover," I suggested. "At least until we can catch the person responsible."

Alistair nodded at two of his lieutenants, assigning them to escort the politician inside. "It was my opponent, Ramovich," the prime minister continued. "He knows he can't beat me. I have the popular vote. This is just the kind of dirty, murderous tactic he would employ."

He walked away leaving his wife to trail in his wake. With so much going on, I'd barely looked her way, but now that I was, it struck me how mismatched they were as a couple. I would never suggest that physical attributes are all that matter, but the prime minister was, to put it bluntly, short, fat, and ugly. His wife was tall, lean, and elegant. Like an ageing film star, in fact. If pushed to guess her age, I would hedge for late fifties, but she carried the years well. Better than me, at least. I guess his status and power would make him more attractive, plus politicians the world over have to be charming (even if they fake it).

The prime minister was still complaining when the doors swung shut to cut off his voice.

Sidling up to Alistair, I whispered, "Who is he?"

"Radovan Filipovic, my dear. Prime Minister of Molovia. He's been in the papers recently. Not as much as you, admittedly."

My cheeks coloured a little. "Do you think we might have an assassin on board?"

Alistair pursed his lips. "I'm no expert on European politics, but someone fired an arrow on my ship, so we are going to figure out who it was no matter what."

He didn't say it, but we both knew it was my job to find the assassin. I pushed Purple Star Cruise Lines into giving me the job of ship's detective because of incidents precisely like this one. I was going to have to familiarise myself with Molovia and the country's political landscape.

A soft grunt of pain from the deck to our left brought our combined attention back to the wounded woman. The paramedics had just shifted her onto their gurney and were preparing to wheel her away. The arrow stuck out from her left shoulder, buried in the meat where the pectoral muscle meets the deltoid. She was lucky, though I doubted she felt it right now.

In her early thirties, she was short and petite, but also trim and fit-looking in a 'I go to the gym a lot' way. She wore her dark brown hair pulled into a ponytail that fell to just shy of her shoulders. Her outfit was a stretchy top over loose-fitting cargo pants and all terrain boots. It didn't really go with the Australian summer temperatures.

Before the paramedics could get moving, I went to her side.

"Hello. I'm Patricia. I just want to say how sorry I am that this could happen to you here on the Aurelia. It's my job to find out who did it and bring them to justice. I'll have some questions for you later, just routine stuff, but there's no need to worry about any of that now. I need to inform your travel companions, though. They will want to meet you in sickbay." I turned to face the nearer of the two paramedics. "You're taking her to sickbay, right?"

"For an assessment, yes, but this close to the coast, I already know the doctors will want to fly her back to Sydney. Hospitals there will have the facilities to look after her properly."

"I'll ready the helicopter," said Alistair, lifting his radio, but he stopped when the wounded woman objected.

"No! No, I can't go back to Sydney!" She could feel our eyes on her. Her outburst required explanation. "It's … it's not that bad," she said, trying to sit up. She was Australian. It was the first time I'd heard her speak, and the accent was hard to miss.

Both paramedics surged to stop her.

"Whoa there, ma'am. That's a real arrow sticking out of you. Let's not make it any worse by moving around, please."

"It's really not that bad," she argued, though I think she could tell no one was buying it. "Just don't send me back to Sydney, okay? I'll be fine being treated here."

The paramedics settled her back onto the gurney, their soothing voices doing little to alleviate her concerns.

"I just need your name," I went with her when they started toward the doors, "so I can inform your travel companions." I figured she would be with a partner and possibly kids as well. She was the right age to have children in tow.

Her reply came instantly, and she delivered it with a tinge of sadness or regret. "I'm travelling alone. There is no one to tell."

Like Justin, the elderly gentleman I met just a short while ago, she was all by herself. Unusual, but not unheard of.

"Someone at home then? I just need your name so I can contact your next of kin."

The paramedics were going through the doors and their faces made it clear they weren't about to slow down so I could grill their patient. I could go with them, but the security officers sent to check the helipad were on their way back and my job was to catch the archer.

Looking down the length of her body as she lay flat on the rolling bed, the woman said, "Sorry. I have no next of kin, either."

Torn, I let her go rather than chase any longer. I would catch up with her in the sickbay later. There, once the arrow was out and she had drugs to keep the pain at bay, I would find out a little more. Not because I suspected she could be involved in the attempted assassination – the woman was just an innocent bystander – but because she didn't want to give me her name and that was making my skull itch.

Friends

Much as I expected, the security detail sent to check the helipad found very little, but interviewing the Molovian prime minister would help to pinpoint the assassin's location. He claimed to have seen him, but I was already questioning how the archer could have missed.

He or she (the prime minister said it was a man, but I chose to reserve judgement for now) would have been firing down at an angle, but I didn't need a tape measure to know the total distance was less than fifty yards. The Aurelia is a big ship, but it's still a ship, not a city.

I cannot recall ever firing a bow and arrow, though I'm sure I must have at some point in my childhood, but Lieutenant Deepa Bhukari, a former Pakistani Army infanteer and sniper, told me the principles of picking a spot would be the same.

"It was probably here," she said, looking about as though trying to find a reason to challenge her claim. She pointed to the sun. "This part is in shade, which would make them harder to see. Strange that the prime minister spotted them, but I suppose he might have caught movement from the corner of his eye. There's a great view of the main doors leading out from the top deck, and you can see people approaching from inside through the windows. Plenty of time to know the target is coming and be ready." She leaned over the railing in a classic archer's pose. "Set up here. There's not much wind because we are in the lee of the superstructure. Target comes out through the doors, and pop. Impossible to miss."

"But they did miss," I pointed out.

Deepa frowned. "Yeah. I mean, I say impossible to miss, but I guess a seagull could have swooped at precisely the wrong moment. The target could have stumbled. It can happen."

I chewed on my lip. My skull continued to itch, but no longer with regard to the poor woman who caught the arrow. There was something off about the attack. I'm not saying I could make the shot, but looking down at the sun terrace, it really wasn't all that far away.

There was nothing more to learn from where we were and plenty of people I needed to interview. On the way back down through the ship, Deepa said, "I guess it's been a while since you had a case to challenge you."

I let a sad laugh slip out. "It's not the only one. I found a necklace just a couple of minutes before the shooting happened."

"A necklace?"

"Yes. An expensive-looking thing with a ruby the size of my thumb."

"What is it with you and finding gemstones?" She was making light of my recent history and it helped to have some humour enter my day.

"Anyway, I left it with your husband, who probably took it to sickbay. I can kill two birds with one stone if that's the case." I should have predicted Deepa's confused expression and took a moment to explain about the chunk of meat inside the bag with the necklace.

"That's just weird," she remarked. "Why would anyone do that?"

Why indeed? It was the third thing making my skull itch. There would be a reason, but until I could find the time to give it some thought, the necklace and the meat would remain a mystery. Jewels that might have come from a heist were interesting, but no one was going to place them above an attempted assassination.

There was a killer on board the ship. Whether motivated by their personal politics or hired to do the job, they were bound to try again, and that meant I was going to have trouble justifying sleep or anything else until I caught them.

Knowing the target helped; it meant we could secure him away from harm and thus defuse the assassin's ability to finish the job. However, it was too early to make any real plans. My priority was to find out more about the prime minister, who his political (or other) enemies were, and who they might have put on board to eliminate him.

A quick check confirmed the leader of Molovia occupied one of the upper deck suites. Heading there allowed me to pop into my own suite to check on the dogs. Barking erupted the moment I opened my door.

The Windsor suite is the finest on the ship and has to be described using terms such as palatial and opulent. Originally intended to house royalty when they came aboard, I have permanent residence due to my benefactor, the Maharaja of Zangrabar. Thanks to him I will never worry about money again and all because I stumbled across a sapphire stolen from his country thirty years earlier.

I crouched to pet Anna and Georgie. It's that or have them climb my legs.

"Yes, yes, girls. I am very pleased to see you, too."

Jermaine, my butler, protector, and best friend in the world, waited just beyond the suite's small lobby. He possesses an uncanny ability to know when I am coming through the door. Very rarely do I ever find him not waiting for me. He took my jacket and enquired about my walk.

"Ah, yes." When I left the suite, I did so to take my dogs for a walk. I regaled him with the necklace tale and the attempted assassination.

"Were you in any danger, Madam?"

Jermaine is a six-foot four-inch muscular Jamaican man who fakes a British accent because he believes it makes him sound the part. Acting the role of a quintessential butler from a bygone era, he is ramrod rigid in his need to address me and everyone else as formally as possible. He serves high tea at four o'clock, wears tails in all climates, and will only break character in moments of extreme danger.

His question was to do with his desire to keep me safe. We share an entirely platonic love for each other, and he would get very Old Testament if something were to happen to me that he could have prevented.

"No, sweetie. I was never in any danger."

"Can I offer madam a beverage?"

I flicked my right arm out to check my watch. There was plenty to be getting on with, but nothing that couldn't wait ten minutes. The ship had a security team, and they were still searching for the archer. Not that I believed they would find him or her. They were also protecting the Molovian prime minister.

"Perhaps a pot of tea," I suggested. The planet did not revolve around me or my ability to solve a crime, so to heck with the rest of the world, I was going to take some time to sit with my dogs.

They followed me across the suite to a couch where they bounded up and onto my lap, one attacking from each side. I made sure to fuss them equally and was still fending off tiny dog kisses when the door to my suite opened again.

A mass of spandex-clad blonde bombshell bounced in.

"Hey, Patty. I hear someone got hit with an arrow. The Patricia effect is back." She grinned.

Barbara Berkeley, AKA Barbie, is a twenty-three-year-old gym instructor and Jermaine's BFF. If all the good-looking in the world comes out of one pot intended to be spread around everyone, she was not only first in line but fell headfirst into it. Her body defies belief, her breasts, given that she is lean and athletic, are bounteous and bouncy, her face is that of a cover model, her teeth are perfectly white and straight, and her blonde hair could grace every shampoo bottle on the planet.

Like every other woman on the planet, I ought to hate her, but on top of everything else, she is annoyingly nice.

She also likes to tease me and her comment about 'the Patricia effect' was a dig at my habit for being where the trouble is. I am a trouble magnet. There, I said it. It just seems to know where I am going and makes sure to get there ahead of me.

Surprise, Patricia! Here's a triple homicide for you to unravel. Surprise, Patricia! How about a priceless art theft combined with organised criminals trafficking exotic animals?

I scowled at her. "It is not funny, Barbie."

She settled into the chair opposite my couch just as Jermaine arrived with a silver tray.

"Tea, Madam."

Barbie flashed Jermaine a smile before returning to our conversation.

"Schneider told me the archer missed their target and got some poor bystander. He didn't know who the target was though."

"Radovan Filipovic," I supplied. "He's the prime minister of Molovia."

A frown flirted briefly with Barbie's brow, and she withdrew her phone. "I know that name."

Jermaine picked up the teapot. "Prime Minister Filipovic has been in power for a decade amid rumours of election fixing and other scandals. He is expected to lose in the upcoming general election in a few weeks' time."

Barbie and I both looked at him.

"How do you know all that, sweetie?" I asked.

He poured my tea with one hand behind his back. "There was a column in the Times, Madam. I read about it last week. He is very much in the news, it would seem. The columnist was of the opinion that he is holding back his country's economic growth and has only stayed in power this long because he has manipulated the press."

Barbie pulled a face. "No wonder someone tried to kill him."

"And they will probably try again," I muttered around a sigh. I checked my watch again and felt guilty about taking a few minutes for myself. What if the arrow missing was a clever misdirection, and the killer knew the prime minister would end up back in his suite? What if the suite was loaded with explosives and set to blow, killing everyone inside?

I held my breath.

"Patty? Are you okay? You've stopped moving and you look worried."

PRIME SHOT

The pulse inside my head became audible as I starved my brain of oxygen.

With a gasp, I sucked in a lungful of air. No explosion came.

"I was just thinking," I explained a little weakly. "What if the miss was on purpose?"

Barbie sipped her tea. "Why would anyone do that?"

I picked up my cup. "Good question."

Mystery Guest

With my teacup empty and no acceptable reason to stall any longer, I was about to head to the prime minister's suite when Lieutenant Commander Martin Baker called my phone. Radios are the standard method of communication for the crew, but we handle a lot of sensitive information that is often best not shared with everyone else.

Phones also allow us to keep our conversations private from the rest of the crew.

"The meat is beef," he reported. "It looks like a nice piece of sirloin."

Curious, I asked, "How can they tell?"

A polite laugh sounded in the distance at Martin's end. I could tell it was Dr Hideki Nakamura, the ship's most junior doctor and Barbie's boyfriend.

"If a doctor cannot tell when they are not looking at human flesh, they ought not to be a doctor."

"Sorry, Patricia," Martin apologised. "I should have said you were on speaker."

"That's okay." I dismissed his concerns and moved on. "It's good news. That's all I care about." I did not want to discover there was a mad butcher on board with a partially carved up victim. "Did you get anywhere with the necklace?"

"I haven't had confirmation yet, but I think the old gentleman you were with might be correct. I was able to contact the police in Sydney and sent them a photograph of the item. When Bingley's respond we will know if it came from their boutique or not."

It was hard to imagine how I would manage without my team to back me up and support me. In Martin's hands the mystery was on its way to being solved. Of course, I hoped the necklace would not be from the heist in Sydney as that created a new problem I would have to solve.

For now it was a problem only in potential and could be ignored.

"Move the necklace to a safe for now then. You're still in sickbay, I assume."

"I am."

"How is the patient?"

"The woman with the arrow wound? Dr Davis is about to operate, but I think … hold on. Here's Dr Nakamura."

"It's a simple enough procedure for once, Patricia. The arrow missed her arteries and lodged in the muscle. All Dr Davis has to do …" he explained the procedure in what felt like painstaking detail though I expected he'd abridged it significantly.

"So, she'll be fine?"

"She'll have a scar, and won't be playing cricket anytime soon, but she's young and fit … we all expect a full recovery."

Now that Hideki had finished, Martin spoke again, "There's one more thing you should know."

"Oh?"

"She's given us a false name."

I blinked, recalling how coy she'd been when I tried to get it before.

"But you identified her through central registry?" I doubted Martin would reveal the information unless he had the answer as well. However, when he spoke again, his tone of voice sounded like he was scratching his head.

"Well, yes," he replied cagily. He clearly had something more to reveal.

"Go on." I huffed out a slow breath, deflating my upper body while I questioned why nothing could ever be easy.

"She was reluctant to give me her name and kept saying she wanted to remain anonymous without providing a reason why that would matter. When I persisted, she told me her name is Sonya Cage, but there's no one by that name listed as a passenger. I could have pushed her further but chose to find it myself instead."

"So her real name is?"

"Stephanie Morris and she's travelling alone. I can grill her about why she lied, but I want to check her accommodation first."

Cruise ships attract people with money to spend and that attracts criminals of every flavour. She could be a pickpocket, a con artist, a prostitute, a card sharp looking to get clever in one of our casinos. Or she might be completely innocent. There was one good way to find out.

"Where is she staying?"

"Cabin 1278. Want to meet me there?"

If I went to the prime minister's suite I would get stuck there for an age. In the minute or so I spent in his company I could tell he was the kind who makes demands and negotiates everything. He would have questions about my investigation before I had even had a chance to start it. I needed to get to him as soon as possible, but my itchy skull dictated my next move was to check out Stephanie Morris.

Concealed

The Aurelia is arranged over twenty decks. The bottom six house the freshwater tanks, storage for bulky belongings being moved from point A to point B, fuel, the engines, crew accommodation ... it's a long list, but the passengers cannot access them. They get the rest of the ship where the cabins range from small to large to ridiculous. We cater to all budgets and supply our passengers with restaurants, shopping, entertainment, and activities of all shapes and sizes.

A cabin starting with a twelve would be on deck twelve – obvious really, and I had been on board long enough now to have learned my way around. I got there ahead of Martin who would have changed elevators in his journey from the sickbay in the 'crew-only' area.

I knocked and listened. Listed as travelling alone does not rule out the possibility of accomplices. Teams of pickpockets have plagued the ship more than once. However, when no reply came, I used a universal key card to open the door. It used to be that I ran around with a stolen one and will admit I got into a fair bit of trouble for using it before the cruise line recognised my value. Now I have one of my own, just like the security officers. I also have a radio just like them, but I do not have a gun.

You might think that foolhardy, but I am not a fan of firearms in general. The first time I fired one I almost wet myself. There are always security officers to hand, and my unarmed policy hasn't resulted in my death yet.

I let the door swing inward, knowing it would reveal a mid-sized cabin with a porthole in the far wall. Dominating the main room was the bed. It was a queen that was yet to be slept in with a suitcase on top. Stephanie, if that was her real name, had not yet opened her suitcase to unpack, or was the tidiest unpacker in the universe. A quick look in her closet confirmed it was the former not the latter.

"Anything?" asked Martin, breezing in through the open door.

"I just got here. But no. Not yet."

I checked in the small shower room to be sure there was nothing hidden there, but in less than ten seconds it became obvious the only item in the room was the suitcase. I've never been a fan of going through other people's private possessions. It feels invasive at an almost intimate level, but I understood the necessity. Besides, if we could rule her out as a person we needed to watch, I could focus on other tasks.

Martin was ahead of me, his right hand already clad in a latex glove. He added another to his left hand and gripped the suitcase zipper.

My breath caught when he flipped Stephanie's luggage open like a clamshell, but there was nothing inside to warrant my trepidation. Neatly folded clothes, items of underwear, and shoes filled one side. Toiletries and more clothes filled the other.

"Oh. Here we go," Martin's hands were rummaging over and through Stephanie's belongings, objectively seeking anything that might raise concern. He was doing his job and being thorough, but I had not expected him to find anything.

I leaned a little closer when he pulled a plastic club from under a pair of jeans. Fifteen inches long with a small amount of flex, it would do the job if employed against someone.

"Self-defence?" I hesitantly asked, trying to think from the standpoint of a woman travelling alone.

Martin placed it on the bed and continued to search the suitcase. He found nothing until he reached the toiletries. Concern piqued by the presence of a weapon our metal detectors would not identify, he unscrewed or removed every cap to sniff the contents. I said nothing, though I thought it to be overkill and was shocked when he snatched his face away from a perfume bottle.

"Pepper spray," he rasped, choking on the little he'd inhaled. It clearly bothered his nose, so I employed caution when I took the bottle from his outstretched hand to test it for myself.

I've never smelt pepper spray, but I have burned spices in my skillet at home and the effect is much the same. The concoction caught at the back of my throat and seared the inside of my nose even though I'd kept it away from me and hadn't even sprayed it.

"Wow." I fished around in my bag for a tissue.

The perfume bottle full of harsh chemicals joined the club, but Martin found nothing else. Still, it was enough to demand we question her with extreme prejudice. She smuggled not one but two weapons onto the ship, and it was my job to find out why. Had we found the tools of a thief, no further explanation would be necessary. Without them, I questioned what nefarious purpose she might intend to employ them for.

The answer came as a surprise.

Sisterhood

"He will kill me if he finds me," Stephanie sobbed. She was out of surgery and recovering in sickbay where she expressed she at least felt safe. "I have tried to get away from him before, but he always finds me and forces me to come home."

"How, Stephanie? How does he force you to return to him?" She was an abused wife on the run from her husband. It made my heart ache that anyone could suffer like that. I knew it happened, but could not understand why she would return to him.

"Because if I don't, he will kill me," she sobbed, her words broken as she tried to get them out. "But it's worse than that. He always said he would go after my mother if I ever left him, and I know he would do it. He's sadistic."

I had no words I could find to offer comfort.

Using her uninjured arm, she fumbled around to get her phone out. "I probably shouldn't show you these," she mumbled, looking embarrassed. "But they tell a story." She navigated to her photographs and turned the screen so I could see it.

The picture was of her upper half. Wearing only a sports bra, she was lying on a hospital bed not too dissimilar to the one beneath her now. The entire right side of her ribs were a mass of bruising.

My voice came out as quiet as a breath. "He did this?"

I got a nod and watched a single tear roll down her cheek. She scrolled to the next picture and the next, each one showing a different part of her body covered in bruises or stitches.

Putting the phone away, she said, "My mom died a few weeks ago. Cancer. He doesn't know. I hid it from him. It was the one thing he knew he could always hang over my head. I didn't even attend the funeral." The sadness she encapsulated with her words brought tears to my eyes as well. "But I had a plan, you see. It was what my mom would have wanted." She lifted her head to meet my eyes. "It was your story that gave me the inspiration."

A little taken aback, I said, "Me?"

She smiled for the first time in minutes, her eyes brightening even through the tears.

"I read about you in the papers months ago. It was after that thing in Zangrabar with the Maharaja."

There were several interviews following my escapades there, most of which I wished I'd never given. It didn't help that at the time I was most famous for a photograph one happy snapper caught of my underwear when I fell backwards off a stage.

"You ran away to sea to escape your husband, too. That's right, isn't it?"

Not exactly. I ran away from a situation I refused to face, not violent abuse. However, she was no longer sobbing and in talking about my exploits, her voice now had an upbeat edge. I wasn't going to quash it.

I said, "Close enough. It changed my life. He won't be able to get to you here, you know. You'll be quite safe without the defences you brought on board." I opted not to use the word 'smuggled' in reference to her weapons. They had been removed and would not be returned. I could see no reason to make more of it than that. "Do you have a plan for when you leave the ship? A place to go? A destination in mind?" From my limited experience reading about women in such terrible circumstances, I expected to hear she had no money put away and very little by way of long-term plan.

"I'm getting off in Hawaii," she said. "That's all the passage I could afford. I was able to get a temporary work visa. I'll find work there, even if I have to live rough or in some kind of hostel for a while. I just need to get enough money for the next part of the plan, which is to get to Europe."

"Do you have family there?"

The hint of a smile faded. "No. I don't have any family anywhere. It's okay to be alone for a while though. Anything would be better …"

She didn't finish the sentence and I could see she had retreated into herself again. The pain she felt left deep scars she might never fully erase and in that moment I knew I was going to do whatever I could to help her. I had money she could use to set herself up, but that would only ever be a temporary fix. Freedom, in every sense of the word, would come only when she could support herself.

"You could stay on the ship," I suggested. When she looked up with hope in her eyes, I added a point I believed would seal the deal, "He won't be able to get on board, Stephanie. I can put a blocker on his name so Purple Star won't sell him a ticket and the security guards monitor everyone trying to get onto the ship. We can find you work, even if it is only until you have enough money to move on."

In truth, I didn't know if we could do that at all, but I would wager my ability to sway Alistair if I posed the question at the right time. Like when we are in the shower, perhaps. The captain of the ship could find a way to 'off the books' employ Stephanie if he wanted to.

Tears brimmed in Stephanie's eyes once more. "You would do that for me?"

I placed a hand on her forearm. "I'm not sure what I can achieve, but I will do my best. For now, please just believe you are no longer going through this alone. I am here to keep you safe and make sure you can restart your life in a way that will ensure he never comes anywhere near you again."

I could feel Dr Davis hovering behind me. He allowed me to speak with her so soon after surgery, minor though it proved to be, because she brought weapons onto the ship, but he was clear of my need to be brief. Rest would do her good, as would the confidence I hoped my promise to help might give her.

With a wish that she recover quickly, I withdrew to find Martin waiting outside.

"You heard that?"

He nodded. "No wonder she wanted to arm herself. Do you want me to investigate her husband? See what I can find out?"

"Yes, please. I fear I am now somewhat overdue at Prime Minister Filipovic's suite."

"Yes, he seems the type to kick up a stink if he feels his concerns are not taken seriously."

I huffed out a frustrated breath and started walking. Martin kept pace at my side. "Obviously, his attempted murder will get my full attention. If for no other reason than we have a dangerous passenger on board." There were other reasons to want a swift resolution, among which were bad publicity and the very real concern the assassin's aim might be better next time.

It was getting to be a long day, and I wasn't nearly done yet.

A Friend in Need

On my way back to the top deck, my phone rang. Expecting to see the name of one of my team displayed on the screen, I was surprised, yet pleasantly so, to see 'Felicity Philips' instead. I first met Felicity when she organised my wedding more than three decades ago. It would be wrong to say we stayed in touch, but we were friendly and ran into each other on occasion simply due to proximity – she lived not so very far from me.

My wedding was the first for a fledgling business she started, but it grew and then some. A few years down the line she was known as the person to go to for all the bells and whistles. Her clientele were pop stars, TV personalities, and people with more money than they knew what to do with. To really put a cap on her career, she recently landed the contract to run the next royal wedding, held in Canterbury Cathedral in just a few months.

"Felicity," I smiled to greet an old friend. "Everything all right in England?"

"Hello, Patricia," she replied in a tone that killed my smile. She was on edge and hearing it made my pulse quicken. "I cannot speak for the whole of Blighty, but I'll cut to the chase and let you know why I am calling."

"Fire away."

"I am going to have to talk in code a little. I'm under strict instructions not to reveal anything to anyone."

Now she had my interest. I mean, you can't be a sleuth if you don't love a mystery, and her need to be cryptic ticked all my boxes.

"Just a moment." The elevator stopped on deck eighteen, the doors opening to let half a dozen passengers on. It sounded like our conversation was not one that ought to be overheard, even if the subject at hand would be discussed in code. I angled my right shoulder sideways to slip out as the passengers tried to get on.

They were looking at me in a way I am getting used to. My face is recognisable, but few can instantly place where they know it from. Not so this time because one lady in particular yanked her partner's sleeve and whispered urgently that, "It's her! It's her!"

I hurried away.

Safely separated from eavesdropping ears, I found a spot out of the way to resume our conversation.

"Right. I am ready. What do you need from me?"

"Well, if you can do it, I need you in England four weeks from now. Twenty-six days, to be exact, though you might benefit from being here a little earlier."

I logged the request and mentally checked my calendar.

"I will need to tell my employers why I am returning to England." Actually, I probably only had to tell Alistair, but he would want to know why I felt compelled to leave my post on the ship again.

"Ah. So this is where I have to figure out how to tell you without telling you. There is something happening in four weeks that isn't scheduled to happen."

"If I said Tonbridge Wells or Berkshire, would I be on the right lines?" There is no such place as Tonbridge Wells unless you look on a map. Locals such as Felicity and I know it as Royal Tonbridge Wells because that's what it says on the signs when you drive into it. Berkshire, a county in the middle of the south part of England likewise carries the 'Royal' prefix.

"Yes, Patricia. How clever. Indeed. So that is happening in four weeks' time and I fear I need your particular skills to address an issue with the ... um."

"Security?"

"Yes, security is as good a word as any."

"Is there a specific concern?"

"Um, okay. How do I say this? You may have seen in the news that several people from Tonbridge Wells are no longer with us."

I translated her sentence in my head: there had been deaths in the royal family recently.

"There is some concern they might not all be accidents."

I sucked some air between my teeth. A month ago, when I was still in England, Felicity mentioned in passing her concerns for the royal wedding and the recent (mostly) untimely deaths from within the royal family's ranks. I could only assume it had escalated. She needed me back in England and I was going.

"I will be home as soon as I can."

Felicity sighed with relief. "Thank you, Patricia. I cannot tell you how comforting that is to hear."

"There's a few things to figure out here first, and that's going to take me a couple of weeks, but I will be with you days, if not a week, before it all gets underway." I would make it right with both Alistair and Purple Star or quit if I had to. The royal family was under threat, and I was being asked to help keep them safe. I felt like I was wearing a union flag as a cape.

I promised to stay in contact and that I would tell no one about the unannounced change to the royal wedding. Felicity sounded stressed and I wanted to ask why, but she needed to clear the line and make other calls. I let her go with a further promise that I would be there to lend a hand. That she wanted me for my ability to figure out if the royal family were in genuine jeopardy or not, was never openly expressed, but I doubted she wanted a hand arranging the flowers.

Call complete, I hurried back to the elevator. It was now more than an hour since the prime minister of Molovia suffered his near miss; a long enough time that I ought to have been there already. I worried he might be kicking up a fuss, but when I turned into the passageway leading to his suite, I encountered a bigger problem.

Politician Through and Through

People filled the passageway, blocking my path, but it took me less than a second to correct my assessment. They were not people at all; they were reporters. I could see their recording devices, cameras, and tablets. Crowded around the prime minister's door, the hungry newshounds were baying for his story, and I could hear him giving it to them.

"... dirty, negative tactics, that is my opponent's chief tool in his campaign against me. He recognises that I am the better statesman, the one the world takes seriously. He wants to lead Molovia not for any lofty hope that he can improve life for the average person, but to fuel his own political hunger. That is why he sent an assassin to kill me today."

I drew closer, sneaking up to the rear rank of those gathered around his door. Peering between heads I could see into his suite where a video camera mounted on a tripod recorded his delivery. Now dressed in an impeccable black suit with waistcoat and sombre tie, he even looked like a politician.

Not that I have anything against those who make decisions and lead democracy. Not at all. I think they would all make perfectly good firewood.

PRIME SHOT

My thoughts on the subject notwithstanding, I was shocked to see so many members of the press in attendance. What's more, they appeared to be eating up his words. When the press trap me and I have no choice but to talk to them, I get heckled. They ask invasive, unfair questions and point out I have neither jurisdiction nor authority to conduct my investigations anywhere other than on the Aurelia. They would be correct if I were attempting to operate as a law enforcement officer, which I do not. Nor do I make arrests in any of the places I visit, though I must admit Jermaine has restrained a few miscreants here and there.

"What of the reports that you had an affair with the daughter of your foreign minister, Bianca Vladinova?" asked one of the reporters stationed just outside the door.

The prime minister never took his eyes off the camera, but he bristled visibly at the question.

"Thank you for raising the subject. It is one that must be addressed." He twisted at the waist to look to his left and held out his hand for his wife to join him. She now wore an elegant yet informal dress with a jacket and a simple necklace of pearls.

She crossed the room to take his hand in hers.

"For the record," the prime minister continued now that the optics were correct, "I have only met Bianca Vladinova once in my life. It was at a cocktail party thrown by her father when she was eighteen. Together with my wife, we were the guests of honour. What you are witness to with this ugly rumour is yet another example of my opponent employing dirty tactics to muddy my name and turn voters against me."

"But there are pictures of you exiting a hotel, prime minister," challenged a different reporter.

This time the prime minister smiled a knowing grin and looked at his wife again. "Well, we all know how easy it is to manufacture pictures using artificial intelligence these days. I dare say I could generate an image of me leaving the same hotel with Minnie Mouse if you gave me a few minutes."

His comment brought a round of laughter. These were the friendliest and least bloodthirsty reporters I had ever seen.

"Thank you, ladies and gentlemen of the press. Thank you for attending this impromptu address. The people of Molovia deserve to know the truth. As you know, this is my first holiday in years, so it should come as no surprise that Lisik Ramovich would see my absence as his chance to seize some initiative. He will not prevail, though. I will not let him. Carry that word to our people."

Pinned in his suite, he should have needed to retreat to one of the bedrooms to escape the reporters, but with his last words still echoing in my ears, I watched them pack up. I backed away, surprised they were yet to notice me and certain they would have questions the moment they did. However, they dispersed, some going in the opposite direction, some going around me as they departed the prime minister's suite.

Silently, I berated my inflated ego. Not everyone would always want to talk to the great Patricia Fisher, and I shouldn't think otherwise.

When the cameraman and his assistant left, carrying their equipment over their shoulders, I stepped up to the door and knocked politely on the frame. The suite's butler, a man called Castle, was about to close the door.

"Mrs Fisher," he addressed me and turned to speak with his principal. "Sir, the ship's detective is at the door. Do you wish to see her?"

I felt my lips tighten but refrained from pointing out that I was going to question the prime minister regardless of his opinion. I rarely have to enforce it, but maritime law gives me a lot of clout for those occasions when I require it.

"Yes, of course," the prime minister sounded cheery and not at all concerned that it took me so long to get to him. "Mrs Fisher, is it not? My apologies for not recognising you earlier. I was," he chuckled, "a little distracted."

"That's perfectly all right," I replied, meeting him halfway across the room as he came to shake my hand. I heard the door close, Castle doing his job as efficiently as any of the Aurelia's butlers.

"How are you, sir?" I wasn't sure how to address him. Prime Minister was too much of a mouthful and first names didn't feel right given that he is a head of state. "Is your wife okay?" I peered around him.

His wife was helping herself to the medicine cabinet, as I like to call it.

Castle hurried to intervene. "Let me get that for you, Madam." Jermaine wouldn't let me pour my own drinks either.

"We're both a little shaken, but unharmed, which is the only important thing. Unfortunately, in the modern climate, all too many political activists believe they can create change with force. Can we offer you a drink?" He turned his body toward the kitchen, inviting me to join him and his wife where Castle was mixing a cocktail.

Could I justify a gin and tonic? Did it count as calorie intake if Barbie didn't see me drink it. No, I absolutely could not, and I decided there and then I was going to abstain to keep my head clear.

"Just a small Hendricks with slimline tonic," I said, wondering how the message in my brain got lost on its way to my lips.

"With cucumber, Mrs Fisher?"

"Naturally. Thank you, Castle."

There were a dozen questions I could lead with, but one was bothering me more than the others.

"Where is your security detail? Were they called away?" The last I saw of the prime minister was his back vanishing inside the ship with a glut of the ship's guards around him. They were supposed to be guarding his suite and it shocked me to find no sign of them.

"Oh, I sent them away, Mrs Fisher. There was really no need for all that fuss. I'm sure the assassin won't be foolish enough to try again so soon after a botched attempt."

"I'm afraid I cannot agree with you, sir. Additional security is necessary at this time. I shall recall them."

The prime minister held up his hand to stop me. "I really must insist, Mrs Fisher. My wife and I are on holiday. Our first in years. I refuse to let bullying tactics scare me into staying in my cabin, lovely though it is."

I couldn't stop the shock registering on my face. "You intend to walk around as though nothing happened? What if the assassin tries again?" I glanced at his wife, who looked as worried as I believed she ought to be. "At least allow us some time to catch whoever fired the arrow. They are on this ship; of that we can be sure."

"Perhaps we should take her advice, dear," his wife voiced her opinion for the first time.

The prime minister was not inclined to listen. "And do what in the meantime, darling? Hang around in our room? Take a long bath and watch some TV? I hardly think so. I am paid to lead my nation and that is not a task I can do in hiding. The country will know that I refused to be cowed by my opponent's attack dog. They will see my fortitude, my courage, and my strength, and they will know I am the person they need to lead them into the future."

He'd dropped unprompted into speech mode and was actually quite good at it. He spoke boldly and with conviction, but here's my problem with politicians: they are narcissists. A narcissist believes their opinion is the right one and will argue and argue until others back down and let them have their way. They are charming, but they use that power for their own gain, rarely for the benefit of others, and they will never admit they are wrong until there is no other option. Do you think heads of charities invented spin doctors? No, spin doctors came about to find ways to make politician's lies sound justified.

Regardless, I could tell he wasn't about to back down. In theory I could confine him to his suite, essentially placing him under house arrest, but that would cause a mushroom cloud to explode over Purple Star Cruise Lines and I would be found with my finger on the big red detonator button.

"Very well, sir. I cannot stop you from venturing where you will, but please allow me to provide security. I have a team of my own I can …" I trailed off as he raised his hand to stop me.

"That won't be necessary. I have my own security with me, Mrs Fisher."

"Really?" I felt my forehead creasing. "Where was he earlier? I don't recall seeing him on the sun terrace."

The prime minister smiled like only a politician can. "You are indeed observant, Mrs Fisher, and thoroughly deserving of your infamy as a sleuth. I saw no danger and stood him down. I believe he went to the spa." He chuckled as though his security guard attending the spa was funny.

I was lost for words, which people who know me will say is quite unusual. We had an assassin on the ship and we knew the target, but I couldn't convince the prime minister to take any precautionary measures that might keep him safe. A lone security guard would do nothing against a determined assassin.

But what was I supposed to do?

Perhaps sensing that I was floundering, the prime minister turned his body toward the exit.

"Thank you for checking on us, Mrs Fisher. I shall be certain to pass my gratitude along to your captain. Don't let us keep you, though. I'm sure you'll want to get on the would-be assassin's tracks."

He had his left arm out to guide me from his suite and Castle was already moving to get the door.

Prime Minister Filipovic thanked me and wished me luck again before I found myself unceremoniously deposited back into the passageway outside his suite. I hadn't even sipped my gin and tonic.

An Old Friend Comes to Stay

A fugue state gripped me so completely that I was inside my own suite and talking to my dogs before I realised I'd walked around the top deck to get there. Anna and Georgie were on their backs rolling for tummy tickles, which my hands performed on autopilot because my brain needed to continue with its train of thought.

The last few weeks had been so peaceful and undisturbed one could be fooled into thinking the role of a ship's detective is close to pointless. Then, in the space of an hour, I found what I suspected to be a stolen necklace, landed in the middle of an assassination plot, and met a woman running for her life.

The necklace was going to have come from the heist my new friend Justin mentioned. I just knew it. Even so, it remained the lowest priority of the three. I wanted to throw my efforts into helping Stephanie, yet I knew my priority had to be the assassin, even if the prime minister did act as if the attempt on his life was of little concern.

Why was that? Most people would be scared. No, they would be terrified. Had we instantly caught the assassin, I might downgrade that to rattled simply because the danger would have passed. His wife was worried, but the prime minister had a spine cast from titanium. He said it would make his country vote for him, but was that it?

"Your coat, Madam?" Jermaine hovered, waiting for me to finish with the dogs.

They rolled onto their paws the moment I took my hands away, mother and daughter trotting back to their favoured position on the couch closest to the kitchen.

I let Jermaine take my coat and shucked my shoes. They are comfortable, but taking them off is a relief, all the same. Crossing the room barefoot, I spied a gin and tonic on the kitchen counter.

"Is that for me?" I asked, hoping that would be the case.

"No, sweetie," said a familiar voice. "It's mine. But you can have it. Your marvellous man will make me another, I'm sure."

Strolling from one of the suite's unused bedrooms – it used to be Barbie's, but she moved in with Hideki full time when we got back to the ship – was none other than Lady Mary Bostihill-Swank. She had a cocktail glass in each hand.

"Mary!"

"Yes, dear, tis I." She took a healthy swig from the gin and tonic in her left hand so she could place the glass on a low table and wrap an arm around my shoulders. "Hello, dear. I hope you don't mind me dropping in unannounced like this."

"Not at all. Why didn't you say you were coming, though?"

She took her arm back, releasing me so she could sip from the glass of refreshing liquid in her right hand. Sipping is not something I have ever really seen her do, but I chose not to question it.

PRIME SHOT

"What kind of surprise would that be?"

Jermaine was already in the kitchen fixing two more glasses when I lifted the spare one from the counter.

Lady Mary clinked her glass against it. "Cheers, darling."

Now I understood the sipping. She didn't want to toast with an empty glass.

"Are you here alone?" I looked around her to see if her husband might still be in the bedroom.

She tutted and sighed. "George is on another of his terminally boring book tours."

Lady Mary had more money than most people could count and married a man with none. He then went on to become a global bestselling mystery and thriller writer, though I doubted the fortune he'd amassed came anywhere near his wife's holdings. Lady Mary owned a zoo among many other things.

"His latest release has been snapped up by one of those awful streaming services. They plan to make a miniseries out of it and wrote him a cheque with far too many zeroes at the end if you ask my opinion. How anyone puts value on the nonsense in that man's head is beyond me."

Thankfully, Lady Mary was at least vocally supportive when George came within earshot.

"Now, it will be dinner in an hour or so, which means we need to get cracking if we are going to finish that bottle of gin before we go for cocktails."

If you ask people to describe my titled friend, most would start by calling her a lush. Lady Mary, however, would correct them. She has money, and in her eyes it means her drinking makes her a socialite. Quite how one small woman can put away quite so much alcohol without her internal organs exploding I have no idea, but that's what she does.

I took a mouthful of the heavenly liquid, revelling in the icy cold flavours it delivered, but left the rest in the glass when I put it back on the counter.

"I'm afraid I have work to do, Mary. There was an attempted assassination today and the assassin is still on board. I am required to expend maximum effort figuring out who it is and make sure they spend the rest of their cruise in the brig."

"That sounds terribly boring, Patricia. Don't you have people to do that for you? Where is that …" she rolled her eyes toward the ceiling, tipping her head back to consult her memory. "Baker!" she snapped her finger. "And Schneider. Where are those two? They can find your assassin while you and I drink the bar dry."

"Sorry, Mary. Tempting though that sounds," it really didn't, "my duty is to the ship and the passengers on board. I could never forgive myself if someone else got hurt because I took the evening off."

Lady Mary rolled her eyes. "Oh, very well. But I want nightcaps later. What do we need to do first?"

My Team

At her insistence, I took Lady Mary with me when I left the suite to liaise with my team. We have a room of our own on deck ten, a place where we can inspect evidence, discuss investigations, and interview both witnesses and suspects. We like to call it 'The Nest'.

Jermaine came too. His duties for the day were done as I planned to eat on the move. That should mean he had the evening off, but he always claims he has no other purpose in life beyond his need to protect me and meet my every whimsical desire. I allowed him the time to change from his butler's livery and was not shocked to find him dressed as *Steed* from the *Avenger*s. It is his go-to outfit of choice.

I swiped the lock with my key card and the three of us went inside to find my team hard at work.

As well as Martin Baker from Ireland, Schneider from Austria, and Deepa Bhukari from Pakistan, there is Anders Pippin, a small but whippet fast chap from South Africa, Molly Laurie who used to be my maid when I first moved into the Maharaja's house, and Sam Chalk.

Sam has Downs which gives him a unique view of the world that has enabled us to solve cases more than once. He is a ray of sunshine and I have known him since birth as I went to the same junior school as his mother, though I was a year above her.

I got a round of greetings upon entering the room, and a chorus of surprise when they spotted Lady Mary. That she still had a gin and tonic in her hand derived no remarks – they were used to seeing her with a drink. Not seeing her with one might have stood out as unusual.

"Three cases," I said. "Who's doing what with which?"

Nominally, I am the head of the team. I am the detective; they are my officers. However, in reality, it is Martin who assigns them tasks ninety percent of the time. He is the senior rating and letting him do so frees me up to let my mind explore the mysteries we face.

If asked to describe how I solve a case, I would not know where to start. The answers just sort of arrive in my head. That can take hours or days depending on the nature of the crime, the person or people behind it, and how well they have hidden their movements. To find the answers I expose myself to as much information as possible and somewhere inside the old grey cells, as *Hercule Poirot*, my favourite literary detective, would say, the answer forms.

Martin reported, "I'm looking into Stephanie Morris with Molly. We have a photograph of her husband already."

"He looks like a real tosser," said Molly, never one to mince her words.

Ignoring her, Martin asked, "How much do you want us to do? This started because she got hurt, but she was just an innocent bystander. You intend to help her out, I know. So beyond making sure her husband cannot get to her while she is aboard, what do you want us to do?"

I sucked some air through my nose. "I'm not sure yet. Please find out as much as you can about her husband."

Molly poked the computer screen to her left. "We've compiled a file for you to read at your leisure."

"Thank you. Unless you think you have more to uncover, please leave it at that. As Martin said, I intend to help her." My feelings for the poor woman were strong. They made me wish there had been a version of me to help when I first came on board at the lowest point of my life. "Just to get her back on her feet. That's all. She deserves a shot at happiness."

"Here, here," said Lady Mary, emptying her glass and looking around for somewhere to put it. I'd explained the case to both her and Jermaine on the way down through the ship.

"Okay," said Martin. "That leads us to the steak and the ruby necklace. "Schneider?"

Schneider patted Sam on the shoulder. "Give your report, Ensign Chalk."

Part of my deal for taking the job on the Aurelia was that Sam came with me. At thirty-one he'd never had a job until I took him on as my assistant. That was back when I opened and briefly ran a private investigations business at home in England. I hadn't been looking for an assistant, but Sam somehow gravitated into the role, and it stuck. When I abandoned the business, which is now run by Mike Atwell, a former police detective sergeant, Sam came back to the ship with me. I always felt it was a PR exercise for Purple Star to give him a uniform and a rank, but Sam could not be happier.

Why fight it?

Schneider, the giant Austrian, has assumed a kind of big brother role even though he is a couple of years younger. He is paired with Sam most of the time, the two of them working well together.

Sam had to fight to stifle the goofy grin that adorns his face day and night so he could be serious for a moment. "We found contact details for Wallace Bingley's and sent them a photograph. It's out of business hours now, but we hope to get an answer by the morning, Mrs Fisher."

Sam is the only one of the team who still calls me that. I have given up trying to convince him to stop.

"Then we reported that a necklace had been found so all the passengers will get a message on the TV screens."

Schneider cut in with, "They have to dismiss it to make it go away, so if anyone on board did lose it, they will know we have it."

"But we didn't describe it," said Sam. "We didn't want lots of people trying to say it was theirs."

"Good thinking." I gave him a verbal pat on the head.

Sam's eyes rolled up and right. He was trying to recall what else he needed to tell me.

Schneider leaned down to whisper in his ear.

Sam's grin returned. "And we sent the picture to Interpol and the Canadian police to see if it was something they recognised." His smile fell, but only for long enough for him to twist his head so Schneider could confirm he'd covered everything. I couldn't be sure, but Sam appeared to be even smilier than usual. In fact, now that I thought about it, he'd been floating around with a skip in his step for a few days. I was going to have to ask him about it at some point.

PRIME SHOT

"That leaves the assassin," said Deepa. "The team that the captain sent to the helipad didn't pass anyone and could find no sign a door had been forced. It's off limits, as you know, so would have been hard, but not impossible, to access."

Anders picked up where she left off. "I've been looking into Prime Minister Filipovic. He's not what one might call popular at home, but the story of the attempted assassination is already breaking. What's strange is that they have footage playing already."

Stunned, I said, "Show me."

Expecting my request, Anders had a tab open on one of the computers.

The others had seen it and hung back so Lady Mary, Jermaine, and I could squeeze in tight to watch. A voice in the background spoke in the tone of someone recording a home movie. The footage, captured by a passenger I assumed, showed the sun terrace. The camera panned from left to right, sweeping across the swimsuits and bikinis on display until it reached the door where it paused.

Two seconds later the prime minister stepped out with his wife leading the way. He then paused, taking in the view, but doing so blocked the door, forcing the person behind him to stop in the doorway.

That person was Stephanie Morris and I had to watch her get hit with the arrow. It took her backwards, flooring her just as she nudged her way around the prime minister.

The rest of the footage was unwatchable as all hell broke loose and the passenger with the camera lost his focus.

"How long has this been up?" I asked.

"We found it an hour ago when I started researching."

Mental calculation made it clear the passenger with the camera wasted no time selling their footage. It would be impressive were it not so mercenary.

"You've watched that a few times, yes?"

Everyone in my team nodded and Martin said, "We all have."

"Did you get anything from it?"

Deepa said, "No, but I want to track down whoever took it. They were panning from left to right and there's a chance they caught the assassin getting into position. Depending on the quality of the footage, we might be able to see a face. We just need the whole film."

Boom! Just like that we had a huge lead. If it panned out.

"Where are we with that?" I asked.

Martin stepped in. "Well, we have started reaching out to the media firms showing it, but getting them to reveal their source is a long shot. We're nowhere with that yet, but I wonder if you making an appeal would get a better response."

I saw what he was saying. "You mean like over the ship's tannoy or something like that?"

"However you want to do it. If they come forward with the footage ..."

I nodded, thinking. "I'll get right on that when I leave here." I would go directly to the bridge and get the request out this evening. Catching our mystery archer in less than a day appealed enormously.

"As I was saying a moment ago," Anders continued, "the PM isn't exactly popular in Molovia right now. The polls place him way behind his main opponent, but I found one report that suggests this will completely swing things around. Much of his campaign for re-election has been mired by negative issues highlighted by the opposition party."

That reflected the PM's claims. He'd called it negative campaigning, or something like that. Rather than highlight why they should vote for Lisik Ramovich, they told people why they shouldn't vote for Filipovic.

It made me want there to be a third box that offered 'None of the above' as a choice.

"The PM's people in Molovia are calling the assassination attempt the desperate last play of a man who knows he's going to lose. Of course, Lisik Ramovich denies any involvement," Anders finished.

I allowed myself a moment to think before responding with my thoughts.

"Okay. Here is how I see things. The necklace is neither here nor there until we find out where it came from. If a passenger dropped it, which I find highly doubtful, we can return it. Otherwise, it is almost certainly stolen. For now, there is no need to give it any further thought. I will take on Stephanie Morris myself. There is no case here beyond making sure she recovers and can move forward with the confidence that her husband won't be able to get to her even if he does find out where she is. I'll read through your report tonight, thank you. Our focus has to be not only on finding the assassin but in preventing a second attempt on the PM's life. He is refusing additional security."

I got a chorus of disbelief from everyone in the room.

"I know. It's crazy, right? He believes there will be no second attempt and is determined to enjoy the cruise with his wife. However, he hasn't met any of you …"

"Plain clothes covert bodyguarding?" asked Molly, her eyes alight with excitement.

I smiled and nodded. "Just so."

Never the lady, she pumped her fist into the air like a footballer scoring a goal and roared, "Yeah, baby! Ooh, can I go first?"

Martin's voice instilled a little calm. "We will tackle this in pairs. We will be armed, and we will be guarding the PM whenever he steps out of his suite. But," he made the 'but' a big one, "we must remain undetected. I think we should let Mrs Fisher go …" he swung his eyes my way to make sure I was done and got a nod in return, "so I can draw up a hasty roster so we all know who is doing what."

I left them to it, content the PM would have additional security watching his back and the vantage points around him while he wandered the ship. It wasn't enough, not by a long shot, but unless the captain overruled the prime minister's wishes to insist he have security, which I very much doubted he would, then it was the best I could do.

The video footage remained my best hope, and with that in mind, I aimed my feet in the direction of the bridge.

Address the Ship

Lieutenant Crispin snapped out a salute as I approached the elevator to access the bridge.

"Crispin," I sighed. "You don't have to salute me."

"But you hold a rank, Mrs Fisher," he replied, looking confused while his arm dropped back to his side.

"Yes, but only on paper. I have no uniform. I have no training, and everyone calls me Patricia. Why don't you try it?"

His cheeks turned pink. "What, like now?"

I made an encouraging face. "Yes, Crispin. Give it a go. Nothing bad will happen."

"Okay ... Patricia," he said, nervously looking around in case someone might have heard.

"You can salute me if you like," said Lady Mary, slurring the 's' of salute slightly.

The elevator arrived, Crispin using his key card and then a keypad to enter an eight-digit pin – a recent security addition – to make the car move. He also radioed to inform the guards on the bridge that we were coming up.

Alistair wasn't there, which came as no great surprise. He spends a lot of his work time touring the ship to make sure the passengers have everything they need and to make them feel special. The job of actually running the ship is delegated to the deputy captain, of which there have been many since I first came on board. One was shot, one was sacked, one jumped overboard before he could be arrested for murder and secretly returned with a plan to send the ship to a watery grave. Like one of those Energizer Bunny adverts, Commander Ochi had lasted longer than the rest of them combined.

"Mrs Fisher, what brings you to the bridge?"

I explained about the video footage of the attempted assassination and made my request. Sixty seconds later I had a microphone in front of my face and a dry mouth.

"Anyone got a glass of water?"

"I have some rather nice Irish whisky?" Lady Mary offered a hip flask from her pocket.

A glass of water appeared and I used it to wet my lips. I wouldn't say public speaking bothered me, but I was about to speak to the entire ship, and it was making me feel on edge. Perhaps because I have a habit of being a klutz. Not that I could trip over my own feet on the radio, but sticking my foot in my mouth raised its unwanted head as a distinct possibility.

Commander Ochi indicated he was ready to go. I gave him a thumbs up.

PRIME SHOT

To announce the imminent message, a jingle played – this is a cruise ship, not a warship.

Gripping the microphone, I pressed the 'send' button. "Good evening, passengers, this is Patricia Fisher, the ship's detective. As you may know there was an incident on board earlier today in which an attempt was made on the life of the Molovian prime minister. Please be assured we are working flat out to find the person responsible." I paused to breathe before plunging into the request. "One of our passengers was able to capture video footage of the incident and it is that person to whom I now appeal. Please identify yourself to any member of the crew so that we might be able to examine the full recording. Thank you, passengers, and good evening."

Commander Ochi said, "I'll have that message repeated on the TV screens around the ship and in the passengers' rooms. Hopefully, though, the passenger is already tugging on someone's sleeve to let them know they are the one."

"Hopefully," I echoed. There was no reason to hang around on the bridge, especially since Alistair was elsewhere. I thanked Commander Ochi once more and took my leave.

In the elevator, Jermaine asked, "What is your dinner plan, Madam?"

I needed to eat something. That I could not deny, but it wouldn't do to be seen relaxing at one of the ship's many restaurants, not with an assassin on the loose, and I'd asked Jermaine to take the night off. He would happily race around the kitchen making me whatever I might request, but I didn't need anything lavish.

"I think I'll make myself a sandwich, actually. I need to read my team's report on Stephanie Morris and be ready to review the footage when our mystery passenger identifies themselves." The thought prompted me to check the radio in my handbag. It was on and tuned to the right channel, so the passenger was yet to come forward.

They could have missed my message amongst the hubbub of conversation if they were out to dinner, or there could be dozens of other reasons why they were yet to make themselves known. It would become my highest priority task the moment they did, so perhaps the delay was a good thing – I wanted to focus on Stephanie.

Master Criminal

Justin Masters relaxed in front of his TV with an old film. In his right hand, he held a small glass of sherry, his preferred tipple. Not that he was much of a drinker. He found it dulled his mind, but a small amount every now and then wasn't going to hurt.

Not at his age.

Today's meeting with Patricia Fisher was his first. It took planning and precise execution, plus a little luck to place the bag with the necklace where he believed her dogs would find it. He wasn't a dog person – they made too much noise and were messy. He liked cats, and wished he'd brought his along on the trip. However, dogs were predictable and that had worked in his favour.

He smiled to himself as he sipped his sherry. The clever line he delivered, suggesting the necklace might have come from the recent heist, was the clincher. Little clues like that would determine if she really was the opponent he wanted to find. Would she be able to figure out he was behind the crimes?

He boarded in L.A. six weeks ago at the same time she did. Not that she noticed. He was just another passenger, another old man. There would be no reason to ever speak with him, but he needed to not only make her acquaintance, but become someone inside her circle of friends.

In many ways this amounted to tipping his hand, but if she never knew to look his way, what would be the point? Only once she was on the hook and actively trying to catch him could he claim victory by stealing from under her nose and slipping silently away.

If she was half the detective the papers made her out to be, the necklace would show her the trail. He arranged a bank job in Sydney where the team he assembled were able to empty the vault without tripping the alarm. Discovering the empty vault became the breaking news story right when the Aurelia sailed away from the Australian coast. It wasn't the first since he came on board. In Bora Bora a different team hit a series of billionaires' homes, stealing art in the form of oil paintings and sculptures and he had already lined up another job in Honolulu.

Justin planned to work his criminal magic in every single port until Patricia Fisher finally realised it was a show put on for her. Only once he had her attention would he tease her with the final act – a heist on board the Aurelia itself.

He knew his target and he knew Patricia Fisher would be watching it like a hawk.

There was still much to do, but he was in no hurry. Justin took another sip of his sherry and thought about the next part of his plan. Patricia's team was far too tight knit. Disrupting them wasn't necessary, but wouldn't hurt in the long run.

He would do it gradually, targeting those closest to her to ruin her ability to concentrate. When he played his hand, he wanted her to know precisely who she was up against and yet be able to do nothing about it. Not then and not afterward either. The robbery would take place under her nose, but there would be no way for her to catch him, no clue she could use to bring about his arrest.

PRIME SHOT

His infiltration started a week ago when he arranged for a talented actress to come on board. She had a very simple job. A job for which she held all the appropriate qualifications. Indeed, she'd wasted no time in meeting her mark and getting to know him.

He almost felt sorry for Sam Chalk.

Sandwich

Jermaine didn't fight me for once, so I got to make my own food. It's hard to explain how such a mundane and simple task can be missed, but cutting slices of cheese to add to the ham made me feel like a domestic goddess. I added tomato slices, crisp lettuce leaves, and a thin layer of mustard. With a mug of tea, I wandered back to the desk with my dogs dancing along by my feet like two moving trip hazards.

They were not used to seeing me in the food preparation area and were most interested in what was on my plate.

"It's not for you, girls."

They looked at each other and then back up at me, their expressions suggesting I must have gone completely mad.

I bit into the sandwich, revelling in the simplicity of its flavours. Speaking around my mouthful as I chewed, I said, "Seriously, ladies. You had your dinner two hours ago. There's nothing now until bedtime biscuits."

The mere mention of the 'B' word made their tails wag in expectation. I rolled my eyes and grabbed the mouse.

PRIME SHOT

The suite comes with a computer for my use. I have a laptop I use whenever I am mobile, but Barbie is a bit of a whizz with a computer and did something that means I can access all my files wherever I am through a thing called the cloud. I know the term, but don't ask me to explain what it is.

Navigating to my emails, I opened the file on Stephanie and began to read. Anna and Georgie watched until the sandwich was gone, then slunk across the carpet to glare at me from the couch.

The file gave me background information, listing where she went to school, when she got married, and her address in a suburb just outside Surfer's Paradise on Australia's Gold Coast. I had just been there, solving a case with Darius Kane, the Australian version of Tempest Michaels. The report also contained information on her husband, but reading through the file I was surprised to learn he was American, not Australian. I made a mental note to ask Martin to dig a little deeper, though to be fair, he probably had that in mind already. His current employment listed him as a librarian and, if the report was correct, his education focused on literature. He didn't have a criminal record, but Molly was right that he looked ... well, I chose not to employ the word she used.

He looked a little thuggish, truth be told. An American football star through high school and college, he was broad across the shoulders and listed at six feet and six inches tall. Short cut sandy brown hair and deep-set brown eyes made me believe he would be handsome enough when he smiled and he was clearly good looking or charming enough to win Stephanie's hand. Why then choose to treat her so badly?

Violence in relationships was something I would never understand, but I knew there was more to it than use of physical force. Partners can play mind games too, be obsessively controlling, overly critical, and employ many other terrible tactics when they were supposed to be giving love and support.

There was no criminal record, but seeing their address made me reach for my phone.

It was the same time in Australia as it was on the ship – we hadn't gone far enough to leave their time zone yet, so I found his number and pressed the green button on my phone's screen.

It rang and rang and rang off. Before voicemail could activate, I thumbed the button to try again. I wanted answers. Getting the help Stephanie needed could be achieved on board the Aurelia, but only if I could show it to be necessary. A little evidence gathering ought to do the trick, so when the call rang off for a second time, I thumbed the button yet again.

This time it connected and Darius's rich voice filled my ear.

"Patricia? Did you forget something?"

I laughed. "No. It's not that." I explained about Stephanie Morris, her situation, her injury, and what I hoped to do.

Darius was straight to the point. "What do you need me to do?"

"I believe her husband has no criminal convictions."

"I believe that happens a lot more than people realise in these cases."

"Yeah, me too. I know you know a few people at your local police station. Can you call in a favour? I want to know if officers have been called to their address. If I can show evidence to corroborate her story, it will help me to help her."

"I can do that. Give me a few hours. I might have to wait until morning to speak with someone who will feel inclined to help, but I'll get back to you as soon as I can."

PRIME SHOT

I thanked him, bade him goodnight, and hoped to hear from him sooner rather than later.

The night was still young, but I wasn't about to join Lady Mary for a drink. She stopped at the first bar we passed on our way back from the bridge and was likely to be in there for some time. I could catch up with her later, but right now I wanted to know how my team was getting on.

Radovan Filipovic was out and about on the ship, tempting his assassin to try again. Two of my team would be watching, but that wasn't as reassuring as one might think.

A text message confirmed where I could find them, and with the dogs leading the way, I set out again.

Attempted Murder

A cool breeze blew along the deck carrying moist sea air with it. Churning through the Pacific on our way to Hawaii, it was warm enough even in January that I could get away with just a light jacket to keep the worst of the chill away from my bare arms.

I have trained the girls to use an indoor potty, much like a cat, but they still need regular exercise so I walk them around the deck a couple of times a day. If I asked Alistair how many miles of passageways and deck there are he would probably give me an exact answer. All I know is there is enough to satisfy even the most determined walker.

This was a quick stroll to give the dogs some fresh air before heading back inside the ship. My destination was a French restaurant called Frank's on deck seventeen. Despite its reputation, I am not a fan of French cuisine and had only eaten there on one occasion.

I much prefer the Italian place opposite. They are both to be found in an area designed to look like a typical European town square. The deck there is made to look like old, worn cobblestones, the restaurants have awnings as though to protect their patrons from the sun or rain, and tables spew from the fake buildings into the street. It's all very tasteful and elegant and with eight places from which to choose, is always the busiest spot for dinner when the ship is at sea.

Exiting one of the ship's many elevators, I stood to one side to observe. Food smells filled the air, competing and combining to fill my nostrils with temptingly delicious dishes from around the world. Passengers and off-duty crew were enjoying themselves and relaxing. I wasn't looking at them, though.

I trained my eyes to the deck above, searching for the assassin. Not that I had the first clue what he or she looked like. However, anyone standing still by themselves would stand out. Especially if they were holding a bow.

Rotating until I had checked the full one hundred and eighty degrees without finding anyone looking even remotely suspicious, I lowered my eyes.

Frank's French bistro lay straight ahead across the fake town square. The Molovian PM was in there somewhere enjoying his evening meal and the company of his wife.

Taking out my phone, I called Molly.

"I can see you outside," she whispered into her phone. "I'm going to raise my arm so you can see me."

Squinting into the restaurant's interior, I had to scan from left to right to find a hand in the air. It looked just as though she were calling a waiter, and one came.

"Can we have some more water, please?" she asked at a normal volume before whispering into my ear again. "The PM and his wife are finishing up their meal. I mean, they are on the coffee already, so we expect them to move shortly."

Would they go back to their suite or onto a bar or show or even a casino? Given his stubborn refusal to lie low, I fully expected him to continue risking his life for several hours.

"Who are you with?" I asked, wondering who Martin paired her with. Stopping to have dinner was a clever move that placed them right next to where they needed to be.

"Anders," she whispered back. "Martin said we would look natural together."

The two youngest members of my team had been dating almost since Molly came on board.

I told her I would hang around to see where they went next and crossed the town square to view the area from a different angle. If I were an assassin, where would I want to be? That was the question I set myself. Deepa was the right person to answer it, but there was no time to get her here now if the PM and his wife were almost done with their dinner. Besides, she deserved time off, just like anyone else.

Passengers strolled by in every direction, none of them paying any attention to me as I turned my back on Frank's and looked outward. Even though the restaurant had no walls to separate it from the square, the PM would have to leave through the entrance. It was that or force his way between the tables and he wasn't slim enough to pull that off.

To me it meant a sniper with a gun, crossbow, or even a throwing knife, if they were that good, would know where to be looking. However, the ever-moving crowd of passengers going by would block the target from view.

The decks above us, visible because the ship was open all the way to the stars at this point, offered an angle that overcame the people-in-the-way hurdle, but added distance and would make it hard to know the target was coming until he stepped into the street.

PRIME SHOT

Trying to figure out how an assassin might strike had my pulse racing. I felt on edge, so when someone tapped me on the shoulder I squealed in startlement. I also spun on the spot to face my assailant.

"Goodness, Mrs Fisher," said Radovan Filipovic. "It was not my intention to scare you."

The dogs were trying to climb his legs, checking him for treats no doubt, not fending him off in case he really was attacking me.

Sagging as my legs wobbled from the sudden fright, I said, "That's perfectly all right, sir. I was miles away."

"Are you going in?" he asked. "The food is splendid."

I decided to come clean, hoping it might jolt him into accepting the danger to his person had not gone away.

"Prime Minister, I am here looking for your assassin."

Again, his wife took on a look of terror while the PM acted as if he was bulletproof.

"You worry too much, Mrs Fisher. Whoever it is probably scared themselves silly earlier today. But, as I said previously, I will not be cowed into staying in my room. If you'll excuse us, we have a show to attend."

He stepped around me, dismissing my concerns and my person as irrelevant. It was then that I noticed some of the reporters from earlier. The ones interviewing him at his suite a few hours ago were here now. Not all of them, I didn't think, but enough. What were they doing on the ship in the first place? Was he that much of a story that they booked passage to report on his every movement? Had they suspected his vacation would be eventful?

My attention drifted, leaving the PM and his wife to question the itch at the back of my skull. What was it trying to tell me this time?

Sudden gasps, squeals, and cries of anguish from the decks above brought me back to the here and now with a rush of adrenaline. Looking up I saw what caused the panic and I swear my heart stopped beating. Time stood still. I wanted my feet to move, but they refused.

All I could do was stand and watch as a large dumbbell plummeted toward the PM like a cartoon anvil. In the nick of time, the people in the dumbbell's path surged outward to create a circle devoid of flimsy human life. Some pushed to get clear, the more heroic ones taking people with them. Others simply dived to save their lives, but in the half second of warning, the impact point cleared.

The heavy weight smashed into the deck with a thud that hurt my ears and vibrated through my feet.

Stunned to my core, I turned my head and eyes upward to find hundreds of faces looking down. The assassin could be any one of them. Or they could have dropped it and walked away. Around me, the screams of shock and horror continued to reverberate, drowning out Molly and Anders as they yelled into their radios.

The scene was utter bedlam. In the restaurants, chairs and tables had been overturned as passengers fought to either see what had happened or sought to vacate the area at maximum speed.

Through the crowd of people now rushing in every direction, I spotted the PM. Tears ran down his wife's cheeks as she clung to him. He looked shocked, but his expression was one of defiance and anger. Comforting his wife, he appeared oblivious to the reporters snapping pictures all around him.

I started in his direction but stopped when the last person I expected to see got back to her feet.

"Stephanie?" I gasped. "What on earth ... why aren't you in sickbay?"

Her face was all wide eyes and clenched jaw, and she couldn't take her eyes off the dumbbell.

"Stephanie?"

She showed no sign that she heard me.

"Stephanie!" I touched her shoulder and her head whipped around so fast it ought to have snapped off.

"That nearly hit me," she blurted, the words finding their way out in a rush. "I could have died!"

"Why aren't you in sickbay?" A sling held her left arm up and against her body to reduce the stress on her injured shoulder, but she had changed her clothes since I last saw her and had more colour in her face.

Using her right arm, she levered herself off the deck. I moved to offer a hand, but she didn't need it.

"I discharged myself," she replied, making it sound like an apology. "The doctor wanted to keep me overnight, but I feel fine, and I wanted something better to eat than what they were offering."

Her phone started to ring, the sound coming from the back pocket of her jeans.

I told her, "I need to check on someone else." I didn't name the Molovian PM, but suspected he would be gone if I didn't get to him soon. Now was the time to hammer home his need for additional security. "But stay here. I'll be back soon."

Two of the ship's security guards ran by me and I could see more coming from the other direction. Anders yelled to get their attention – as first on the scene he'd assumed control and would remain in charge until someone senior arrived.

I left him to direct their actions and intercepted the next two before they could reach him. Grabbing an armful of sleeve, I steered them toward the PM.

"This man was the target. Please escort him back to his suite on the top deck."

The PM bristled, "Mrs Fisher, I …"

I cut him off without hesitation. "Operational security. That dumbbell could have hit anyone, sir. It was meant for you, and we already have one injured passenger. I need to get you out of sight, for now at least." I thought for a moment that he would continue to argue and thanked my lucky stars when he closed his mouth and bowed his head.

"Very well, Mrs Fisher. We will do as you ask."

"Thank you." I watched him go and when the next duo of ship's security arrived a heartbeat later, I sent them to catch up and aid his protection. Someone really wanted Radovan Filipovic dead.

"Mrs Fisher!"

I backtracked a few feet to the opening and looked up to find Molly hanging over the railing three decks above my head.

"He dropped it from here! I have a witness!"

I shot my eyes at Anders, who fired back, "I've got things here. Go catch this guy!"

Grimly determined, I set off. Molly's fast thinking might have just eliminated half of the ship as potential suspects. If we had a witness who could confirm a man dropped the dumbbell, it wouldn't give us much, but if they could provide a description at least … With access to the photograph of every passenger using central registry, there was a chance we would identify the assassin.

Jogging because this was not a situation where walking would do, I went to the escalators. They are about as non-dog friendly as a device can get, so I always avoid them when I am out with the girls. Fortunately, they are not exactly heavy, so I scooped one under each arm and stepped on.

As it whisked me from deck seventeen to eighteen, I turned around to face the scene below. With distance, I gained a fresh perspective but would get a far better view from directly above. A frown creased my brow. Shooting a bow at the target was one thing; a person proficient with such a weapon might reasonably expect to hit the target.

Dropping a dumbbell from thirty feet above the intended victim provided no such accuracy. There were people all around, and the distance from the restaurant doors to the spot where the weight smashed into the deck could be covered in just a few seconds. What were the odds they would hit the PM?

Not only that, they would have to know the target's path and drop the weight almost before he was moving. Furthermore, walking around with a dumbbell would be noticed. Surely. It had 'fifty' printed onto each of the hexagonal ends. I took that to mean it was a fifty-pound weight. Easily enough to kill a person if it hit them on the head.

Nearing the end of the escalator, I turned to face my direction of travel, but not before I spotted another thing wrong with the scene below – Stephanie was gone. I'd asked her to wait, but she hadn't.

Her choices were the least of my concerns right now, so I dismissed them to focus on a second attempted assassination in just a few hours.

Description

Arriving at deck twenty, I headed over to where Molly stood next to the railing. At this point of the ship an opening plunges through the decks taking light and sea air to the shops and restaurants below.

She saw me coming and came to meet me. With her at the railing were Schnieder and Sam. Both were out of uniform but must have heard the alarm calls over their radios. A further six of the ship's security team in their pristine white uniforms were keeping passengers at bay.

"He used a pram," Molly reported. "The dumbbell was in it." The pram sat abandoned at the edge of the rail.

That explained how he got it to the railing without people noticing. I could envisage him waiting until the right moment, looking over the edge with his hand in the pram ready. Anyone glancing his way would see a dad out with his newborn baby. The weight would be in sight for a fraction of a second, but someone spotted him anyway.

"Where is our witness?"

Molly pointed. "Over here. He's Australian, so there's no communication barrier. He wants to help but says he didn't see the guy's face."

That was disappointing, but anything he could tell us would help. Plus, I was going to make him look at dozens or even hundreds of pictures to see if he might have seen more than he realised. Seeing a photograph of the assassin might jog his memory.

"Patty!"

I was halfway to the witness when I heard Barbie calling my name. She had Jermaine with her and they were both jogging across the deck to get to me.

"Patty, we just heard. It is right that someone dropped a dumbbell through the ship?"

"Are you all right, Madam? Shall I take the dogs?" That Jermaine's first concern was for my safety came as no surprise.

Handing him the leads, I said, "I am fine, thank you, sweetie. I was never in any danger. And yes," I replied to Barbie's question, "Someone did indeed drop a dumbbell through the ship. I believe it was a second attempt on the Molovian Prime Minister's life."

"It was a fifty, right?"

I opened my mouth and closed it again. How did Barbie know that?

"It came from your gym, didn't it?"

She nodded. "One of the guys noticed it was missing earlier. We figured it had to have been mixed up with the other weights or left behind one of the cardio machines, but we scoured the place and couldn't find it."

"It's an odd choice of murder weapon," remarked Jermaine.

He wasn't wrong.

Molly introduced me to the witness, a man from Adelaide called Shane Toomey. On the cruise with his wife for their tenth anniversary, he took a stroll while his wife relaxed in the bath. He just happened to be passing the railing when the assassin dropped the dumbbell.

Initially, Shane thought the man had thrown his baby over the edge.

"I freaked out," he admitted. "There was nothing I could do, but I ran to the edge anyway. I guess I should have tackled the guy instead."

Shane was in his late thirties and looked capable of wrestling a man to the ground, but taking on a killer was not a strategy I could endorse.

"No, you did the right thing. Tackling criminals is our job. However, you can help us to identify who it was."

He glanced at Molly. "Sorry. I already told Ensign Laurie I didn't catch his face. I was too focused on what I thought was a baby."

"Nevertheless, you can describe what he was wearing, his approximate age, his hair colour …"

"Yeah, I can do that. He was a little older than me, I think. His hair is black, but I recall seeing some grey hair at the sides. He was tall. Like maybe six feet four and he was white. I remember that much." He was surprising himself with how much he noticed. "Oh, and he had on a jacket with a hood, which I thought was a little odd, but now I remember he flicked the hood up over his head as he walked away. That's why I couldn't see his face when he turned around."

This was better than expected and would really help.

"I need to let my wife know where I am first, if that's okay. I didn't bring my phone and I've been out far longer than I intended. Chances are she's already lining up a butt kicking for making her late for dinner." He laughed to show he was making a joke.

"We can certainly compensate your time, Mr Toomey." With a click of his fingers, Alistair could arrange a private sunset dinner on the beach at our next destination. "But I'm afraid dinner will have to wait." I touched Schneider's arm. "Please escort Mr Toomey to our interview room via his cabin so he can speak with his wife."

Schneider asked, "Do you want us to wait for you or get started?"

"No, don't wait for me. Please narrow down the search using whatever Mr Toomey can remember and have him look through passenger photographs. I will get there as soon as I can."

Invited to follow, Schneider and Sam led the witness away. I prayed for a swift solution, but wasn't about to hold my breath.

Barbie and Jermaine were also about to leave when Martin and Deepa exited the ship's superstructure. Martin had the evidence bag over his shoulder. On land the cops would call in a forensic team. Out at sea we get to do it all ourselves. They would dust for prints and check the pram to see if our assassin left anything behind. The search for evidence would likely yield nothing worthwhile, but we had to do it.

I checked they had all they needed and was about to head to the prime minister's suite again when our radios flashed into life.

"Incident on deck fifteen. Port side, midships. Two men chasing a third. Chavez and Doogan in pursuit. Request assistance, over."

Another incident already?

The ship had enough security officers that there was no need to dispatch anyone from my location or disturb those working the scene outside the restaurants on deck seventeen. Others would be closer and could get there faster, but I felt drawn to know more.

Taking my radio out, I held it to my lips. "Chavez, this is Patricia. Can you describe the men?"

"Yeah!" he hollered back sounding a little out of breath. "Two of them look like *Dog the Bounty Hunter*. One black guy one white guy. Both in their late thirties. The guy they are chasing is wearing a hood so no clue what he looks like other than he is white."

Molly eyes met mine, and she said what I was thinking, "That could be the assassin!"

Bounty Hunters

Leaving Martin in charge of the scene on the top deck, I took Molly and ran. Do you see what I was telling you earlier about the need for sensible shoes? On board a cruise ship, I ought never to have to run unless for exercise, but that has never been the case pretty much since the first day I stepped off the gangplank.

Mercifully, we didn't have to run far before Chavez messaged to say they had caught two of the men. The third, the one the other two were chasing, got away. We had a description and officers were looking for him, but I can testify how easy it is to hide from security on such a large ship. I've had to do it myself more than once.

By the time we got to deck fifteen and found them, Chavez and Doogan had been joined by Goldsworthy and Odev, two female security officers, not that I feel there is a need to distinguish between male and female. I only tell you their gender to complete the picture.

When Chavez said the two men giving chase looked like *Dog the Bounty Hunter*, I wasn't sure what picture to conjure in my head. I'm aware of the show but haven't ever knowingly seen it. However, both men wore loose-fitting black jeans with heavy work boots on their feet, the kind one might select if kicking in doors was on the agenda. Their top halves likewise mirrored each other with white t-shirts and Kevlar vests. Bare arms led to fingerless gloves, the same style I'd seen on Tempest and Big Ben. They wore dark sunglasses despite the unavoidable fact that it was night and they were inside. Only their hair and skin colour set them apart. The white guy's dark brown hair was long and shaggy. It fell to his shoulders in the manner of an eighties rockstar. The black guy was completely bald, his scalp shaved so close it looked polished.

They were sitting on the deck, their backs against a bulkhead, but they were not restrained which told me they'd elected to cooperate.

"This is Mason Searle," Chavez pointed at the white guy. "And Edgar Bruner. They won't tell us who they were chasing or why." Jamie Chavez came aboard a few weeks ago as a transferee from another ship. He'd quickly settled into the routine and was good at his job. He was also rather popular with the female crew members due to his easy smile and handsome face.

"We already told you we have a bounty to collect," growled the white guy, his accent confirming he was Australian. "The man is a fugitive from the law. He skipped bail and it's our job to return him to arrange a new court date."

"So you are bounty hunters?"

"That's what I said, isn't it?"

The white guy sure was surly and his companion wasn't giving off happy vibes either.

If they didn't want to be pleasant, I could match them. "Gentlemen, this a cruise ship and we are in international waters. The authority you have on your home soil does not exist here."

"All we have to do is catch him. When we reach Hawaii, we will arrange to fly him back to Australia, where he can stand trial."

"Nevertheless, you cannot pursue or arrest him while he is on this ship. Identify the passenger and I will alert the authorities in Hawaii so he can be arrested when he disembarks."

"Not a chance," spat Mason. "If he gets arrested, we don't get our reward. Booking passage on a cruise ship isn't exactly cheap. This guy is worth a hundred grand to us."

"I will say it again. You cannot pursue or detain him while he is on this ship." I took a moment to consider the issue. With nothing but their word their target was guilty of anything, I still believed they were telling me the truth. Therefore, it was right to ensure justice could be served. "Okay. Tell me his name. If he is a fugitive, we will detain him for you. He can be released into your custody when we reach Honolulu."

Mason pursed his lips, his expression angry, and his partner said, "No. This is our business, not yours. What's to stop you swooping in to claim the bounty yourself, Patricia Fisher."

"That's right," snarled Mason. "We know who you are. Maybe this is how you got famous in the first place. By stealing other people's busts."

I was about done listening to their idiocy.

Turning to Doogan, I asked, "Any sign of the man they were chasing?"

He took a few moments to check with the officers searching the surrounding area, but the trail had gone cold. The ship is a rabbit warren of passageways; the decks stacked on one another to make it just as easy to go up or down as it is to go sideways, forward, or aft. Imagine playing Donkey Kong in four dimensions.

"We could have had him!" snapped Mason, voicing his anger at Chavez and Doogan with a shout. "You cost us a hundred grand tonight. Why didn't you listen when I told you we needed to catch him?"

Chavez and the rest had done their jobs and I wasn't in the mood to hear them be berated for it.

Facing the bounty hunters, I said, "Gentlemen, I will have the officers escort you back to your cabins. You are not required to stay there, but I want them to identify where you are staying and they will perform a search of your rooms to confirm you have not brought any weapons on board." I could see they were going to argue, so I spoke over the top of them. "There will be no further chasing around the ship. If you change your minds and wish to have the man in question detained by the ship's security, we will be happy to oblige, but only after you give us his name and I can confirm he is a fugitive. Otherwise, it will be the two of you who get detained. Am I making myself clear?"

They weren't happy about it, but they got to their feet and didn't bother to argue.

"We understand," said Edgar.

When Mason said nothing, his partner elbowed his ribs.

"Okay," he growled, surly till the last. "I understand."

He said the words, but I wasn't entirely sure he planned to comply.

Body Guarding is Tough

I sent Molly back to the top deck so Martin could reassign her and made my way back to the prime minister's suite. Yet again, I found the way blocked by reporters. This time I forced my way through them, politely, yet firmly, insisting they move aside.

As before, the Molovian Prime Minister was being filmed as he responded to the latest attempt on his life.

His wife glanced my way when I barged into their suite, but the politician's eyes never even twitched.

"... your votes will demonstrate far better than my words, that the people of this great nation will not bow down to bullies. For a second time, Lisik Ramovich has tried to win the election by ending my life. He will try again, and he will fail again, for it is my destiny to lead Molovia into the brightest period of economic growth and stability in its history."

Speech complete, he thanked the camera and crew and reporters for their time and effort, making a big thing out of shaking all their hands.

Watching from the side-lines, I found it strange that none of the reporters had questions for him. I'm no political observer, but I've seen UK prime ministers presenting to the nation. Whatever announcement they make is always followed by a bout of quizzing from the assembled press.

Maybe it is different in Molovia.

The press cleared out, leaving the suite feeling empty.

Empty?

"You let your security go again?" I begged to have the prime minister confirm it was true.

A large man stepped into sight. He was in the kitchen where my angle of view had made it impossible to see him.

"I have security, Mrs Fisher," the prime minister replied in an impatient tone. "The ship's officers served no purpose once they had escorted me back to my cabin."

Unable to believe his nonchalance, I gasped, "There have been two attempts on your life in the last few hours. How close does this man have to get to convince you to take extra precautions?"

"Have you been able to identify the assassin?"

Closing my eyes, I forced calm throughout my body. When I opened them again, I said, "He was seen dropping the dumbbell."

The prime minister's security guard came forward, his right hand extended. "Grigore Volantin. The Prime Minister's hard-pressed bodyguard. You have a description? I need to know what he looks like so I can be on the lookout."

"The witness is working with my team as we speak. If we are lucky, we will identify him and be able to make an arrest."

"And if you are unlucky, I need to know who to look out for," the security guard argued. "Work with me, please, Mrs Fisher." He closed the gap between us and shook my hand. "I'm afraid the prime minister is quite stubborn about certain things. I would like him to stay in his cabin where I can reasonably assure his safety ..."

"And what if this man is so determined he attempts a full-frontal assault through the door, Grigore?" Demanded the prime minister. His wife whimpered with fright and was ignored. "What will you do then? You are not armed. If we corner ourselves, we give him reason to attempt it. If I stay on the move with an unpredictable schedule, he will have to take the opportunity when it presents itself. Far better to keep him on his toes and wait for him to mess up."

"Or to succeed, sir," Grigore replied. "Mrs Fisher is right. You are making her job and mine more difficult than they need to be."

"Difficult? If you want an easy job, Grigore, you should milk cows or deliver the post."

Grigore turned to face me and rolled his eyes. I could see he was having a hard time working with his boss. It was easy to empathise.

"Mrs Fisher," he began, letting the argument with the prime minister drop, "I would greatly appreciate it if you would share with me whatever details you have been able to glean. Is it one man we are up against? Or a team? Anything you can tell me might help to prevent a tragedy."

There was no reason not to divulge what I knew, but all I had right now was a vague description.

"Give me enough time to check in with my team, please. If they can identify who the witness saw, he will be in custody minutes later. Either way, I will share what we know. You are going to stay here with the prime minister."

Grigore sneaked a look at the politician and dropped his voice to a whisper. "I don't dare leave him alone. I've been taking sips of water, so I don't need to use the restroom. My pulse is through the roof, and I won't be able to relax until the election is over."

The poor man.

I took his number and promised to call him when I had better information. For now, the prime minister had agreed to stay in his room. The night was young, but they were staying put. From the icy waves coming off his wife, I guessed the decision to remain in their cabin was hers. At least they would be safe for now and I was going to post a couple of security guards outside their door, whether they wanted me to or not.

Pool of Suspects

I made a note to share my step count with Barbie when I got back to my cabin. It was already an impressive number, and I wasn't finished yet. Back at the nest on deck ten, I gripped the door handle and prayed they had been able to identify the assassin.

They hadn't, of course. Were that the case they would have contacted me, but I asked the question anyway.

"Sorry, no," said Shane.

They had him sitting in front of a screen, slowly working his way through possible matches. Deepa was to his left, operating the computer to scroll the images.

"We have fifteen potential matches so far," said Martin.

Shane's cheeks coloured and he apologised again. "Sorry. I don't want to point the finger at the wrong man."

I told him not to worry and that he was doing a great job, which was true. This was his vacation and time he'd set aside to spend making memories with his wife. I would make sure he was suitably compensated and questioned if I might be able to get his accommodation upgraded to one of the upper deck or nineteenth deck suites. However, right now I needed him to concentrate and find the man he'd seen drop the dumbbell.

Martin confirmed they found lots of prints on the dumbbell and were working to identity them. However, the assassin left none on the top deck railing or on the pram. That left me to suspect the fingerprints on the gym weight were from people using it earlier today. The pram had been identified as reported missing an hour before it was used by the would-be killer. A young couple had left it outside one of the ship's many restaurants rather than wheel it between the tables, and only noticed it was gone when they finished their meal.

Determined to hang around until Shane was finished, I used the time to call Alistair.

"Darling, you have had a busy day."

"I have, haven't I?"

"Did the person who filmed the first assassination attempt come forward?"

I felt my forehead crease into a frown. "No, they haven't." Why was that?

"Oh, well, I'm sure they will. Lieutenant Commander Baker told me you have a witness who may be able to identify the assassin." Alistair always used their ranks.

"That's correct. He is here now, working with my team. We have Ensign Laurie's quick thinking to thank for that. She got to the top deck fast enough to find him before he wandered off. But listen, I have a couple of requests."

"Fire away."

Making sure Shane couldn't hear what I was discussing, I asked about the sunset dinner thing and an upgrade to his accommodation.

"It will be done. I shall organise that myself."

"Thank you. There's another thing. The woman who was shot with the arrow…" I explained her situation and what I wanted to do to help her.

"Patricia, your generosity of nature never ceases to amaze me. If she wishes to remain on board the Aurelia, I am sure we can find a role that will suit whatever skills she has. There are key absences in most departments."

Unbelievably, recruiting people to live and work on a cruise ship is difficult.

I knew in advance what his answer would be, but it came as a relief to hear it. I would find Stephanie and deliver the news in the morning. There was a lot going on, but I would find time to make sure she got the chance she needed to start her life again.

Alistair asked if I wanted company when I finished work and I truly did, even if it was just to see his face and hold his hand for a while, but it was already getting late and he had a busy schedule without having to factor in my needs. We would be ashore in Hawaii soon and could spend some well-earned time together then.

I was just finishing up the call when I heard Deepa announce the supply of men fitting Shane's parameters was now exhausted.

Martin stopped what he was doing to ask, "How many possibles have we got?"

Deepa pushed back her chair and rubbed her eyes. "Forty-seven."

That was a big pool, but not so big that we couldn't do some more investigation on each of them.

Deepa volunteered to walk Shane back to his cabin and once they were gone, the inevitable task of assigning a roster for the night fell to Martin. There was a killer on board the Aurelia, so while we all needed sleep, some of the team were going to have to wait. The forty-seven potentials had to be whittled down and that process could not wait until the morning.

Schneider and Molly volunteered to take the first shift. Deepa and Anders would replace them at three in the morning. It was early enough to make me wince. I volunteered all the same, but was told in no uncertain terms I was to rest my mind and figure out who the killer was.

That is my role.

A call to Commander Jandl, the head of the ship's security team, was all it took to have two officers placed outside the prime minister's door for the night. He probably didn't want them there, but I just didn't care.

Unwelcome News

My restful slumber ended abruptly when my phone rang. It took me a few moments to decipher what the annoying noise was, and then a few more to find the source. By then the caller had rung off, but my phone blasted my eardrums a second later when it rang again.

It was Darius at the other end.

"Hey, Patricia," his deep bass rumbled in my ear. "Sorry if I woke you. I'm on an all-night stakeout trying to catch a home invader pretending to be a werewolf. He's been plaguing one of the suburbs near me. Anyway, I got an answer and didn't want to risk missing you in the morning. Basically, you were right. There are multiple logged calls about domestic violence at the address you gave me, but no charges have ever been raised. I guess he's just another scumbag with a wife too terrified her accusations won't stick."

It was exactly what I expected to hear, but Darius had more to tell me.

"I did a little more digging, because it's you. You said she's on your cruise ship and you were worried he might find out and try to follow her?"

"That's right. I've circulated photographs of her husband, so security will be looking for him when we dock in Hawaii. If he finds out she is on this ship, it would be easy for him to fly there and be waiting for her to get off."

"Well, I've got news for you and you're not going to like it."

I readied myself, wondering what on earth he might be about to reveal.

"The desk sergeant I was talking to ran a search for Dale Morris and it turned out his car has been impounded. It was abandoned at Gold Coast Airport."

"So he *will* be waiting for her in Hawaii. That's kind of good, actually. I think I will call ahead and see what the Honolulu PD can do to help me."

"Um, no, his flight wasn't to Hawaii."

I felt my eyebrows meet in the middle.

"Then where did he fly to?"

"Sydney. That's where you just left, isn't it?"

My mouth fell open.

Stephanie's husband was on the ship.

Wife Beater

It was three in the morning, but I was done with sleep. In my nightdress, I rolled out of bed, found some slippers, donned a gown, and headed for my suite's computer.

Less than a minute later I was looking at the face of Dale Morris. Assigned cabin 756 on the lowest and thus cheapest passenger deck, he had somehow discovered his wife's plans to abscond, found out where she was going, and followed her to the ship. He'd been torturing her mentally, emotionally, and physically for years and wasn't done yet.

Well, I could change that.

I dressed in a hurry, grabbing the first clothes that came to hand. Anna and Georgie watched me with bemused, yet suspicious eyes. They wanted to sleep and worried I might plan to take them with me.

"Don't worry, girls. This trip is just for me." Not that I was going alone. I'm not that brave or stupid. I could call on any one of my team or knock for Jermaine. They would all throw their clothes on to accompany me, but in the dead of the night I could find on-duty officers in one of the crew rooms. They would already have their uniforms on, be alert, and probably bored enough to view my request as something fun to do.

I tucked the dogs up with the bed covers and left my bedroom.

"Madam?" said Jermaine, eliciting a scream from me that accompanied my soul as it left my body. My heart went for a swift run around the inside of my ribcage, mercifully returning to its original position when it couldn't find a way out.

Using the wall to keep myself upright, I held a hand to my chest to confirm my heart was still beating and swiped an arm at him when he came within range.

"Are you quite all right, Madam?"

I levered myself slowly away from the wall, but kept a hand on it in case I got the whirlies.

"No thanks to you. What were you are doing sneaking around in the dark?" I took in his outfit. "What are you doing?"

"Going wherever you are going, Madam."

He had on a dark grey suit and black tie with matching pocket square. On his feet, he wore shiny black oxfords, but had for once foregone the bowler hat and umbrella.

"You are going out, are you not, Madam?"

I squinted at him. "Is there a camera in my room?" There had better not be given what I did in there with the captain every chance I got.

"No, Madam. I am a light sleeper. I heard your phone ring, heard you answer it and when I came to the kitchen to get a glass of water, I saw your light was on and could hear you moving the hangers around inside your wardrobe. I surmised that your call was of some importance and required your immediate reaction."

My squint stayed in place. "You are altogether too perceptive."

"Yes, Madam."

"Come along then. Let's go. I'll explain on the way."

As anticipated, I found a duo of bored-looking security officers in one of the crew rooms, which is little more than a windowless space with a couple of chairs and a table. Shocked to have someone walk in on them, they bounced out of their comfy chairs and looked guilty. Not that they had any reason to. Patrolling the decks at night when everyone is asleep is a security formality that rarely finds a purpose. More often than not, their only task is to guide inebriated passengers to the right cabin. After a certain point in the night there is nothing to do. Hence the crew rooms.

"Horobin and Delany, right?" I cannot claim to know the name of every crewmember, but I interact with the security team on a daily basis. I gave them a cheerful wave. "Good morning, chaps. There is a man on board I need you to arrest. It should be a riskless task, but you have sidearms and I do not."

Horobin glanced at Delany. They were both men in their twenties. The kind who go to the gym a lot and look really good in the ship's white uniform with their bulging biceps poking from their short sleeves.

I clapped my hands together. "Chop, chop, fellas. No time to waste."

My heart still ached from finding Stephanie's husband followed her to the ship. So desperate to remain in control, he booked a flight, bought a ticket, and squirrelled himself away. Had he spent his days watching her? Was he waiting to see if she would meet someone on board? The romance of the ship and the exotic locations we visit are great catalysts for single people to find each other.

What would he do if he saw her with another man? Not that I believed Stephanie had any interest in finding someone new. Finding oneself trapped in a relationship with an utter pig could put a woman off men for life.

Regardless, whatever he had been doing and whatever he had planned, I was about to put an end to it.

Speaking quietly as we walked to the elevators, Jermaine said, "Madam, you do realise you are proposing to detain Mr Morris before he commits a crime?"

That I planned to pre-empt his move was not lost to me. But what could I do? If I waited and he found Stephanie, would he hurt her? Would he do worse than hurt her? I refused to risk it. There would be repercussions for locking him up, but I told myself I had credit with my employers and could afford to burn some standing up for womankind.

Delany and Horobin rode the elevator in silence and tailed us to the door of cabin 756. Pausing in the passageway outside, I turned to them.

"I am going to knock. There is no reason to expect resistance or aggression. Not at first. However, I will inform him that he is to be detained and I want you to be ready to restrain him if necessary. I will step out of the way when he comes to the door. That will give you access. He is a large man," I warned. "Ready?"

I got a thumbs up and with my pulse banging away, I raised my right hand to rap on his door.

"Ship's security, Mr Morris. Open up, please." My voice came out steady and commanding, fuelled by the righteous justice boiling in my blood.

I waited and tried again a few seconds later. I wanted to be loud enough there could be no question he heard me, but not so vigorous that I would wake his neighbours. All the same, I knocked a little harder the second time and raised my voice.

He did not come to the door, but that wasn't going to defeat me. Jermaine hovered to my left, ready to defend me against attack when I took out my universal key card. Holding it a few inches from the lock, I made sure Horobin and Delany were poised. They would go in first.

Mouthing, "Three, two, one," I tapped the key, the light on the lock switched from red to green, and they went through the door.

Search the Ship!

I didn't even need the lights on to be able to tell he wasn't in his cabin. The air had a stillness to it that cannot be achieved when a living person is present.

I flicked the switch anyway, flooding the compact cabin with light. The bed was empty, the covers made, but someone was living here. A magazine lay open on the dresser, a book sat on the nightstand, a bookmark poking from its pages. A man's toiletries occupied the shelf in the bathroom and there were clothes in the small closet.

With four of us in the cabin, it felt cramped, so I sent Delany and Horobin outside to wait while I pulled on a pair of latex gloves. I probably didn't need them, this wasn't a crime scene, but it's good practice and I did it without thinking.

Jermaine retreated to the door, giving me space to work. It would not take long to toss Dale's meagre belongings, and I found his passport almost immediately. It had eight months left to run. I dropped it into an evidence bag, purely for safekeeping, you understand, not because it felt like his metaphorical testicles in my grasp. Not at all, and there's nothing to read into how hard I squeezed it before I handed the bag to Jermaine.

There were no weapons that I could find, but that brought little relief. Dale Morris either had them with him or didn't feel he needed one when he could do plenty of damage with his fists.

Satisfied, but annoyed, I ushered Jermaine from the cabin and closed the door before removing my gloves. Traces of the powder they put in them stuck to my skin. Rubbing my hands together to remove it, I said, "We need to find him, and we need to warn his wife."

Jermaine said, "Is that not the most likely place for us to find him?"

The question hit me like a punch to the heart. He wasn't in his cabin! It was the middle of the night and he wasn't where he ought to be.

I broke into a sprint. Doing so without warning left Jermaine and the other chaps behind, but they caught up to me before I reached the elevators. Impatient, I kept pressing the elevator button even though I knew it would make no difference to the car's arrival time.

It probably took less than thirty seconds before the ping preceded the doors swishing open, but it felt like an eternity. All the while my head conjured terrible thoughts and images. Was he not in his bed because he'd already found his wife? Would we be too late to stop him hurting her again?

Weighed down by my guilt for not seeing the possibility sooner, I urged the elevator to move faster and burst through the doors the moment we arrived on deck twelve.

"Come on!" Once again I left the men in my wake.

I was out of breath by the time I got to cabin 1278, but that didn't stop me from hammering on the door and shouting for Stephanie to answer. I gave that about half a second to work before operating the lock with my universal key card.

The men were each far more capable of handling Stephanie's enraged psycho husband if he threw himself at us, but I had a head full of steam and barrelled into the cabin before anyone could stop me.

It was empty.

Unlike Dale's bed, this one had been slept it. The covers weren't messy though, so the occupant hadn't been in there for long or slept without tossing and turning. It also meant Dale hadn't forced himself upon his wife when he found her.

But he had found her, of that I felt certain. Why else would she be absent from her cabin at this time of the night?

There was no obvious sign of a struggle, and while that was a relief, it did little to calm my nerves.

Pulling out a fresh pair of latex gloves, one of which I ripped in my impatience, I said, "Delany, get on the radio and wake everyone."

"Everyone?"

"Yes!" I snapped, jolting him. Then, more calmly, "Everyone. The whole security team. Do so on my authority. We have a woman on the run from her husband and we found both his cabin and hers empty. In all probability he has her and I want them found before he can do … anything. We can worry about how he found her later. Right now we need to scour the ship."

"That's a lot of ship, Mrs Fisher," Horobin pointed out.

He closed his mouth when he saw the fire in my eyes.

"There are no passengers up at this time, so searching the ship will be easy. He will have her holed up somewhere. Check the storerooms and restrooms. He'll want her someplace they won't be disturbed, so think outside of the box and look places you wouldn't normally look."

In a quiet voice, Delany asked, "Is there a chance he intends to kill her?"

I knew why he was asking. Walk in any direction and soon you will reach the edge of the ship. On the upper decks that means a four-foot-high railing and vast, endless ocean on the other side. Toss someone overboard and who would ever know?

"Get moving," I said, unwilling to contemplate the worst.

It was my second time going through Stephanie's belongings and I felt no better about it this time than the last. There was nothing to find, though. The weapons she smuggled aboard were already locked up below deck in a secure area. They would be taken ashore and destroyed when we reached the next port.

Radio messages filled the air. Delany had alerted the bridge and they would have alerted the duty officer who in turn would have sounded a claxon to wake the crew. All the crew. Almost all of them occupied decks five and six where they had small cabins to themselves. The claxon had never been used during my time on board and was there, as one might expect, for emergency purposes.

But this wasn't an iceberg dead ahead. Just a woman fighting for her life.

Over the airwaves I heard senior security officers barking orders back and forth as they organised everyone into search teams. The rest of the crew, the chefs, engineers, stewards, and more would be allowed to go back to sleep. For now, at least. That could change if the situation called for it.

Knowing I had just pulled the proverbial pin from a grenade and rolled it into the centre of the ship, I lowered myself onto Stephanie's bed and gripped the mattress for support.

I sensed Jermaine coming to me and held out my hand to stop him. Dissolving wouldn't help Stephanie. I had to stay focused and alert, ready to deal with whatever we found.

Pushing myself upright once more, I got back to the task of searching her cabin. But my motions were jerky and uncoordinated, my emotions robbing my hands of the fine control I could expect any other time.

I thought there was nothing to find, but just when I was about to quit, I found a spot of blood on the deck. My breath caught and I stared, unable to move for more seconds than I could count.

It was just one blob, but I could tell it wasn't more than a couple of hours old. It says a lot about my life that I can age spilled blood so easily. Looking closer, I found traces where other drops had been wiped up. Or perhaps smeared by a man's boot when he walked through it.

I couldn't tell.

Jermaine stood out of the way, silently waiting like a sentinel in the passageway outside the cabin. He knows me well enough to see a breakdown coming.

Ripping my gloves off, I stumbled from the suite and into his arms. She was dead, I knew it in my heart. The search of the ship would turn up her lifeless body crammed into a toilet cubicle or stuffed under a lifeboat. We would find her husband eventually and it would be my job to tie him to the crime.

Jermaine held me in his unyielding arms, and I allowed myself to wallow in misery. I should have checked the passenger manifest sooner. Why hadn't it occurred to me that he might follow her?

Because there was no reason to.

PRIME SHOT

The rational side of my brain knew I was being irrational, but it couldn't wrestle back control.

My radio crackled. "Mrs Fisher, this is Delany. We have found something."

Something.

"Tell me." If it was her body, I needed to know before I got to their location.

"Well," Delany took his time as though searching for the right words. "They look like bounty hunters."

Losing My Cool

I closed Stephanie's door and left her cabin as I found it. It needed a full forensic inspection and I could get someone on to that soon, but the bounty hunters were up and about when they ought not to be and something about their mission was making my skull itch.

Also, had they seen Dale or Stephanie? Or Dale and Stephanie? The ship is vast enough that two people could spend a fortnight searching for each other and never cross paths by accident, so it was unlikely they would have seen either missing person.

I had to know, though.

On our way we passed two dozen pairs of security officers. For the most part, though they looked a little bleary-eyed, they were alert and doing their job with professional efficiency. I thanked each pair as I passed them.

The bounty hunters were on deck seven, still dressed as before, still looking surly, and less than pleased to see me again.

"You?" grunted Mason. "What are we being held for this time? We weren't chasing anyone. Chances are he's gone into hiding now and we'll have to wait for him to get off in Honolulu."

"Or you could give me his name and I will lend the weight of the ship's crew to finding your fugitive."

Mason's lips clamped shut.

"Gentlemen, I am already tired of dealing with you. I shall not waste my time asking what you are doing roaming the ship at this time. I think it obvious you are looking for your man and I will repeat that you have no authority on this ship. If you do find him, any attempt to restrain him will result in a trip to the brig for you both."

"What the?" Mason surged forward, but didn't get anywhere near me before Delany placed a hand on his chest and Jermaine stepped in to block his path.

Edgar, the less excitable of the two, said, "Putting us in the brig is fine so long as our catch gets the same treatment. We just need him in custody. Isn't that right, Mason?"

Mason's narrowed eyes continued to bore into mine though the effect he wanted was very much diminished by having to lean around Jermaine.

"Yeah, I suppose. We're just doing our job," he pointed out, proving he didn't understand how little I cared.

Ignoring him, I spoke to Delany. "Can you pull up central registry, please?" All security officers carry a tablet through which they can perform a variety of tasks and access the ship's database of information.

Delany handed me his and I used it to pull up a picture of Stephanie Morris.

"Have either of you seen this woman in the last few hours?"

Something unspoken passed between them and I seized on it.

"If you have seen her, I need to know right now, gentlemen." It was my turn to growl. "Was she with this man?" I switched the photograph for the one of her husband.

"We never said we saw her," Mason replied, happy to shoot me down. I thought it to be a lie and it triggered the little itch at the back of my skull.

"This woman is in trouble," I tried hard to frame my voice so I wouldn't sound desperate or begging, and lost my cool when Mason smirked.

Jermaine had stepped to the side again, but his focus was on the pair of bruisers in bounty hunter garb, not the middle-aged woman he'd sworn to protect.

Sensing my actions could be regarded as unhinged, I went with my instincts anyway and launched myself at Mason's face.

"This is serious!" I screamed. I had hold of his hair before anyone could stop me and was using it to pull his head down so I could knee him in the face. Don't ask me where such vulgar, streetfighter tactics came from. I have never used my knee to hurt anyone in my life. Nor my elbows, feet, or forehead.

Unfortunately, but probably for the best, I didn't possess the strength or gymnastic flexibility to perform the manoeuvre, but I sure shocked everyone present with my outburst. For good measure, I aimed a few expletives in Mason's direction as Jermaine dragged me back.

"That woman is certifiable!" he barked, checking his hair to see if it was all still attached. "I'm done with this. Arrest us or get out of our way. We're not breaking any laws."

Annoyingly, he was perfectly correct, and I could see an embarrassing apology in my future. The drama with Stephanie and my concern for her wellbeing had me about as on edge as I have ever been. And that's saying something.

He wasn't getting it yet, though.

Delany and Horobin were waiting for my nod and when they got it, stepped aside to let Mason and Edgar go on their way. We could hear them complaining all the way along the passageway until they were out of sight.

I straightened my clothes and apologised to Jermaine. "Did I crumple your suit, sweetie?"

He smiled in an amused manner and was about to reply when the radios crackled.

"This is Lieutenant Khan for Mrs Fisher. We've found her."

Public Enemy Number One

Dread ran through my veins like ice and I froze. I didn't know the woman. I'd met her only yesterday, but her story spoke to me at a cellular level and I wanted her to be okay.

Gripping the radio hard so my fingers wouldn't shake, I lifted it to my mouth and pressed the send button. "Confirm status. Over."

There was a pause that couldn't have been more than two seconds, though it seemed to stretch on forever.

"She says she is hungry. Over."

I sagged with relief. She was alive. More than that, she clearly wasn't with her husband. Had she escaped him? Was she savvy enough to have left her room so she couldn't be found? That would mean she knew her husband had followed her, and she gave no indication to suggest that was true when last we spoke.

"Please tell her I am on my way and find the poor woman something to eat."

PRIME SHOT

A flick of my wrist showed the time to be a little after half past four in the morning. I would be tired later, but I wouldn't sleep now even if I could return to my bed. As it was, I had far more important things to do.

Accompanied by Jermaine, I found Stephanie in a similar crew room to the one I dug Delany and Horobin from ninety minutes earlier. She had a sandwich in her hands and a chunk of it in her mouth. She chewed ravenously.

Her left arm was still in a sling, but the colour had come back to her face, so she looked healthier than before. She looked up as we came into the room and fought to swallow what was in her mouth.

"Padicia," she mumbled around her sandwich.

I went over to her table and settled into the chair opposite hers. "You had me worried sick."

Her eyebrows danced, trying to work out what message I sought to convey.

"I thought your husband had you."

Now she frowned in question. "Why would my husband have me? He's thousands of miles aw ..." Her voice trailed off. "He's on the ship, isn't he?"

There was no point hiding it from her.

"Yes, Stephanie. He has a cabin on deck seven."

Some of the sandwich was still in her mouth, but she no longer looked as though she could swallow. The piece in her hand she set back on the plate.

"He followed me. I can't believe it. How did he even know?"

I reached across the table to place my hand on top of hers. "That's something I will ask him once he is in custody."

"You're going to arrest him?"

"The first chance I get. When I found out I went straight to his cabin, but he wasn't there and his bed was made so he never got into it last night. I ran to your cabin and when I found it empty I feared he had found you."

"Oh, Lord. I'm so sorry for making you worry. The doctors gave me painkillers earlier, but they wore off right around when I went to bed. They gave me some more in pill form. I was supposed to take them before bedtime, but I guess I lost them somewhere. Anyway, I couldn't get comfortable and couldn't sleep and after lying there awake for a few hours I started to get hungry. I was on my way to lunch when I got hit by the arrow and just wasn't hungry at dinner time. I guess that's all the drugs they gave me. I went looking for somewhere that might be open, but I couldn't find anything."

She looked and sounded glum, but given her haunted past, Stephanie was taking the news of her husband's stalker behaviour better than expected.

"Listen, though, you mustn't arrest him. It will just make him mad, and that will make it so much worse for me later on."

I had to bite down my first response and come at the quandary from her perspective. In her mind she couldn't escape him. If she could board a cruise ship and sail across the ocean only to discover he was right there with her, what more could she do? Where else could she go to be rid of him?

Giving her hand a squeeze, I said, "Stephanie, he can't get to you. I can arrange for twenty-four-hour security and I have teams sweeping the ship to find him." Okay, so that wasn't strictly true because they were looking for Stephanie and had just been stood down, but it soon would be. "He will be ejected when we reach Honolulu tomorrow and the captain has already agreed to find you a place among the crew."

"Really?"

I found a smile to lift her spirits. "Yes. I don't know what skills you have ... we can worry about that tomorrow, but there will be a job for you, just as I suggested there would be. That can be temporary or possibly even permanent. For as long as you want, at least." It felt good to deliver something resembling good news.

"When can I start?"

"Just as soon as you are well enough. There's no rush though. Like I said, we are scouring the ship and will find your husband. By the time we leave Honolulu you will be free of him, and I know some pretty good lawyers if you need help with the divorce."

She slumped back into her chair and blew out a hard breath. Her eyes were on the table when she said, "This is a lot to take in." Looking up at me, she asked, "How sure are you that Dale is on board?"

"As certain as I can be without having him in front of me."

She thought about that for a while and just when I was about to suggest we make a plan for the rest of the day, a yawn split her face in two.

"I need some sleep," she just about managed to say while fighting to close her mouth. "My shoulder doesn't hurt as much now."

"We should move you to a new cabin."

Her eyes flicked up. "You think he knows what cabin I am in?"

"Let's not find out, eh? I will assign two security officers to stand guard outside your door for now. That way, even if he has some method to find out where you are, he still won't be able to get to you."

"I don't know about that. Two armed guards won't be enough to put him off. Dale has a temper."

I doubted he would try to tackle two armed men, but there was no sense in debating it. In truth I didn't have the authority to station guards outside her door. I have my team and they fall under Martin's command. The rest of the ship's security team have their own chain of command, led by Commander Jandl, but I knew my request would be honoured.

"Let's get you to bed, shall we? We can discuss potential roles and the finer detail once you've had some rest. Come on," I encouraged, getting to my feet, "it will aid your recovery."

Delany said, "We're just coming off duty, Mrs Fisher. If it helps, we can take first watch outside this lady's cabin. Commander Jandl will have someone relieve us soon enough."

"Thank you, Delany. That's very good of you."

Stephanie said, "Those guns have real bullets in them, right?"

I walked with them to the nearest bank of elevators and insisted they take the first one. They were going down. Jermaine and I needed to go up. The day ought to be just starting, but I was many hours into it and very much in need of some breakfast.

Breakfast Chatter

Walking through the ship, the scent of coffee assailed my nostrils, so it was with great pleasure that I caught a distinctly stronger whiff of it when I followed Jermaine into my suite. I'd left my dachshunds in bed, but they were up and alert and ready for their breakfast. They tore across the room to greet me.

Lady Mary looked up at us from her position in the kitchen.

"Early morning escapades?"

I explained about Stephanie's husband, his empty cabin, and the ongoing search for him.

"And you think you can change her fortunes?"

Jermaine filled a coffee mug and handed it to me.

"I do, Mary. I really do. Once her husband is off the ship, she can stay here and sort her life out. A year from now, divorced, and with some money in her pocket, if she wants to leave the ship and settle somewhere new ... well, I hope to give her the chance to do so."

Lady Mary dipped her head at me. "Patricia, you are such a generous person."

I didn't know if that was true or not, but a woman in need came into my life and I just couldn't ignore her plight. Not when I believed it was so easy to help her.

The door to my suite opened and Barbie walked in wearing her usual cheerful smile.

"Hey, everyone. Have you seen the news this morning?" She crossed to the big screen TV in the suite's main living area not waiting for an answer. "That prime minister fellow is all over it."

With remote in hand, she found a news channel and turned up the volume. It wasn't Radovan Filipovic on the screen though, but his rival Lisik Ramovich.

Framed with an ornate and impressive building behind him, which I guessed to be the Molovian houses of parliament, he denied any involvement with the attempts on the prime minister's life. When asked to speculate who else might wish to target the head of the country, Ramovich said, "Anyone who lives here. Everyone seems to be forgetting our current economic position has come at his hands. He claims to be the nation's future and that only he can deliver prosperity, but if that were true, why has he not done it already?"

To my untrained ears, he made relevant points in a calm and rational way, but when the feed switched back to the news anchors in the studio, they showed the sudden swing in popularity. It was all moving toward the prime minister and his bid to be re-elected. Maybe Ramovich wasn't behind the assassination attempts, but he was losing ground all the same.

While Jermaine generously made me an omelette, I called Martin.

"Patricia."

"Has the video footage person come forward yet?"

"No. Not to my knowledge."

I found that perplexing. They would have to be blind and possibly deaf to not know I wanted it. That meant the person was choosing to ignore me.

"Do you think I worded the request badly?" I asked. "Could they somehow think they might get in to trouble?"

"I don't see how they could."

Barbie came to join me in the kitchen, turning the TV down again when it switched to a new story.

I thanked Martin and promised to catch up with him once I'd eaten.

"Before you go," he interrupted before I could disconnect. "I got an answer back on the necklace. It was stolen from Bingley's. The police in Sydney were very pleased to learn that we had it, but curious as to how it came to be on the ship. I didn't tell them we found it in a bag with some fresh steak."

Holding her mug in both hands, Barbie asked, "I want to know how it came to be on the Aurelia, too."

"Wouldn't it show up on a metal detector when whoever it was brought it onto the ship?"

I pursed my lips and thought. "It would, but it's a piece of jewellery and lots of women wear necklaces."

"Not as fancy as that one?" Barbie countered.

"But the guys working security are looking for weapons and other contraband items. If a woman removed her necklace to walk through the scanner, I doubt it would even register. For that matter, a man could have brought it on board. Possibly in the jeweller's box. Nothing suspicious about buying gifts while ashore."

Except it wasn't a gift. It was a necklace worth …

"Martin, I don't suppose you asked what it was worth, did you?"

Martin's voice echoed over the phone, "Two million US when you do the conversion."

Lady Mary flared her eyes. "That's quite a necklace."

It really was, and whoever had it chose to throw it away. Figuring out why was as much a mystery as who, but whichever way I approached the case, I could not escape the possibility that we had a jewel thief on board. One who stole millions in jewels from a single robbery and left the police flummoxed.

I changed the subject to explain my phone call from Felicity.

"EEEEEEEeeeeeee! The royal wedding!" squealed Barbie, getting all excited until a new thought made her face freeze. "Wait, you are taking me with you, right?"

On the spot, I had to admit to giving it no thought.

Barbie leapt from her barstool to grab both my arms. "Patty, this is my one best chance to find myself a prince."

I frowned. "What about Hideki?"

She made a big thing about saying, "Who?"

Lady Mary sniggered. "Having a title isn't all it's cracked up to be, sweetie."

"I'd like to find out for myself, if it's all the same." Barbie hit me with imploring eyes. "Seriously, Patty, it's a royal wedding. Do you know how many of those we get in America?"

I had to think about it for a moment. "Um, none?"

PRIME SHOT

"That's right, Patty. None. And it doesn't have to be a prince. A duke or maybe even an earl will do. Just someone with a small county named after their family and more money than a European nation. Is that too much to ask?"

"Is what too much to ask?" asked Hideki, coming through the door.

"Nothing, babe," Barbie flared her eyes at me.

I could only laugh. "Of course I'm taking you with me, Barbie. We are going there to help Felicity catch a bad person. I need you *and* Jermaine."

"What about Lady Mary?" asked my butler, handing out the omelette's.

"Lady Mary picked up her knife and fork. "Oh, I'll be there anyway, sweetie. I'm a personal friend of Camilla's."

Of course she was.

Wearing a thoughtful face, Barbie asked, "What about Sam?"

I was about to say that I wanted to keep the party small and add that Sam was loving life on board the ship, when Hideki spoke first.

"Is the girlfriend thing a new development? I had no idea he'd met someone."

All conversation stopped. Arriving at the kitchen, Hideki slipped an arm around Barbie's waist and kissed her neck. When he felt our eyes on him, he said, "What?"

Blinking as if that would clear my head, I said, "What?"

Now looking confused, Hideki echoed me with, "What?"

Hardly the most scintillating conversation, I managed to break the cycle by asking, "Sam Chalk? My Sam? You're saying Sam has a girlfriend?"

Hideki's eyebrows danced a jig as his eyes moved from face to face. "Wait, you guys didn't know?"

He got a chorus of, "NOs!" from everyone.

"Oh. Well, he was holding hands with a blonde woman. She has Downs too. I passed them on the way here."

It was a huge revelation. To my knowledge Sam had never had a girlfriend. I could ask his mother about that, but ... wow. My heart felt like bursting.

"Is that why you're here, babe?" asked Barbie.

"No, I came to see Patricia about Stephanie Morris."

I had a piece of omelette an inch from my mouth and a vacuum where my stomach ought to be. With willpower like steel, I held off eating it for long enough to say, "What about her?"

"Well, I'm led to believe you are taking her on as a special project."

I mumbled, "S'right."

"Do you know anything about her past?" Hideki asked the question with enough concern that I stopped chewing. "I gave her a brief examination yesterday and she has significant scarring on her body. I've requested a copy of her medical records, but could see ribs that had healed from a break. One of her collar bones has been broken at some point too. Then she has stitch marks where she appears to have been stabbed ..."

He stopped talking when I held up my hand.

"She is on the run from an abusive husband." That was enough to explain her past injuries to Hideki, but I had to tell him the worst part yet. "He's followed her to the ship."

Barbie blurted, "What?"

"I was up half the night trying to find him. He has a cabin on deck seven, but he wasn't there and hadn't slept in the bed. I think it's safe to assume Stephanie won't be safe until we find and detain him."

"Can we do that if he hasn't committed a crime?"

Barbie echoed a question I'd been asking myself for hours, but I said, "Watch me." If her past injuries were anything to go by, locking him in the brig was the only sensible play.

Our breakfast conversation fell into a lull, and I went back to eating with more than enough to keep my mind occupied. When I was finished and had imbibed quite sufficient caffeine, I retired to my room to freshen up and change. Rolling out of bed so early this morning, I was yet to brush my teeth.

First Name Terms

Voices from the other side of my bedroom door echoed through the walls, but I could not make out what they were saying. I'd showered and changed and was just putting my earrings in when a polite knock told me Jermaine was outside my door.

"Come in." I checked my appearance and stood up to meet him as he came into my room. "I'm done, actually."

"Very good, Madam." He turned around in the doorway to lead me out. Like most days, I'd gone with a casual, smart outfit of jeans, top, and jacket. I was letting my hair grow out a bit, so it hung past my shoulders now. Outside the breeze would blow it around and annoy me, but I had a couple of hairbands in my handbag for such an eventuality. On my feet were Sketchers again. Not only was there an assassin on board we were yet to even identify, let alone find, Stephanie's husband was also in the wind and I liked that even less. All in all, I predicted running in my near future, so comfortable shoes were the order of the day.

Waiting for me in the suite was Castle, the butler from the prime minister's suite. He addressed me as soon as I came into the room.

"Good morning, Mrs Fisher. Prime Minister Filipovic would like to know if you can spare him a minute this morning. He is currently relaxing in his suite."

He was on my list to see early this morning, and it would do no harm to ascertain his plans for the day. I fired a quick text to Martin so he would know to meet me. Jermaine insisted he would accompany me today, so I sent Castle back to his suite with a promise to be along soon, and flicked on the TV.

Jermaine wouldn't need long to change out of his formal butler's livery, but I wasn't in a hurry and wanted to see if they were still running news stories about the election in Molovia.

They were, but I had to find an international news segment to see it. A volcanic eruption in Iceland, a shooting at a school in Denmark, and another death in the British royal family took centre stage, but the story of the attempted assassination was there. I expected to see them rerun the footage of the archer almost hitting his target, but jolted with shock when they showed the dumbbell smashing into deck seventeen. Yet again someone with a camera caught the prime minister at exactly the right moment.

Was it coincidence?

"Shall I shackle the hounds, Madam?"

"Hmmm?" Engrossed in the newsfeed, it took a second for Jermaine's question to register. "Oh, yes, please. They could use the exercise."

Looking tall, handsome, and deadly, Jermaine's dark blue suit went well with his brown shoes and waistcoat. He made me feel underdressed. I would feel much better in a nice dress and a pair of low heels.

Anna and Georgie bounced down from the couch by the suite's largest window and ran to the door when Jermaine jingled their collars.

I took another look at Jermaine, bit my lip, and made a decision.

"Won't be a moment!" I ran back to my bedroom.

Two minutes later, I wrestled the zip of my cute dress all the way to the top and checked myself in the mirror. Next to Barbie I would look like a blonde orangutan. Not that it would matter because other women are invisible when she's in the room. However, the fitted cobalt blue dress floated enough that the parts of me I was less happy with were hidden and the rest of me looked good. It ended just above my knees and still went with the Sketchers I chose to keep on. Finally, I added a white, three quarter length jacket since so much of the ship is air-conditioned.

With a quick check of my pockets and handbag, I confirmed I had all the things I might need, and set off to tackle the day.

Jermaine let me lead the way, holding the girls in check so they couldn't trip me in their constant battle to be in front. A short walk around the inside of the top deck led us to the Prime Minister's suite where Commander Jandl had indeed placed a pair of guards. They looked bored, but alert.

"Good morning, chaps." I waved hello. They were two of the newer lieutenants and both American.

"Mornin', Mrs Fisher," they replied in unison as they stepped aside to let us pass.

To my surprise it was the prime minister's bodyguard, Grigore, and not Castle who opened the door.

"Mrs Fisher," Grigore announced me as came in. I'm not sure what he intended to do, but he moved to get out of my way, but somehow misjudged which way I was going. I bumped straight into him and had to apologise.

We both backed away, and Grigore reversed right into the suite to give me all the space I could possibly need.

The television played quietly on the wall to my right, but coming to his feet, the prime minister switched it off as I entered the suite's main living area. He'd been sitting in an armchair next to the balcony reading a broadsheet newspaper. He placed it on a coffee table.

"Good morning, Mrs Fisher ... may I call you Patricia?" he asked. "I feel like we are working closely enough for us to switch to first name terms." He extended his hand. "I'm Radovan."

"Patricia."

He let my hand go and turned to look out to sea. "Last night scared my wife, Patricia. I suppose the arrow that almost hit me scared her too. She wants to stay in the suite and hide until you have caught the assassin, so I must ask how your investigation is progressing. Are you any closer to catching the man who tried to kill me?"

"We have been able to identify a short list of possible suspects, so yes, we are getting closer. I summoned my security team leader to meet us here ..."

A well-timed knock at the door interrupted me.

"Hopefully that is him now." I paused, twisting slightly at the waist to watch the door. When Martin came through it, I introduced him.

"Prime Minister, this is Lieutenant Commander Baker." I reverted to formal rather than use first names. "He commands my team of investigators. You have the list, Martin?"

"Good morning, sir. Yes, Patricia, I have it right here." With a tap on the screen of his tablet, a man's face appeared. "Can I ask that you please look through these photographs, Prime Minister? We believe the assassin boarded the Aurelia posing as a passenger."

The prime minister took the offered tablet to scrutinise the list of men with Martin and me standing either side.

"If any of these men look even vaguely familiar, please let us know," I encouraged.

The prime minister gave an almost nod of acknowledgement and scrolled to the next photograph. When he got to the eighth or ninth, the face looking out of the screen sent a spasm through my body. The prime minister continued scrolling, and I almost snatched the tablet from his hands.

Dale Morris was among the men identified as a possible match. The witness only caught a glimpse of the man with the dumbbell and most of the matching came from height, skin colour, and body shape, but Stephanie's husband was in the pool.

Did that mean something?

Concentration stolen, I missed the prime minister checking the rest of the forty-seven possibles, only returning to the present when he handed the tablet back to Martin.

"Sorry, no, none of those men are familiar to me. Is this really all you have?" He aimed the question at me.

I didn't hide the truth. "So far, yes, but I believe you can help us."

His right eyebrow twitched in response. "How exactly?"

"The reporters you have following you around. They work for you?"

He reacted as if I'd slapped his face. "No! What on earth would give you that idea? Reporters work for themselves. Or for media firms. They report the truth and, trust me," he wagged a finger under my nose, "they are rarely a politician's friend. I use them to my advantage, just as anyone else in the political arena must, when the opportunity arises."

"Then why are there so many of them on board the Aurelia? Their reporting of the attempted assassination has completely changed your election hopes." It wasn't my intention to accuse him, and really I hadn't meant to, but that was the way it came out. I wanted to withdraw it, but the chance was snatched away by the prime minister's angry retort.

He vibrated with energy being held in check. "I will win the election because I am the better candidate! While my rival stoops to negative propaganda, accusing me of extra-marital affairs, and under the table deals, I continue to represent the will of the nation. The press you accuse me of manipulating are here because they can smell a story like a shark smells blood in the water. I doubt any of them imagined Ramovich would ever stoop low enough to hire an assassin, and you can be sure there will be nothing to trace the killer back to him, but can you blame me for using his failed attempts as the springboard I need to beat him?"

Feeling a little embarrassed, I said, "I wasn't accusing you. The reason I brought them up was to enquire whether one of them might have been the person who captured the footage of the attempts on your life. The footage of the arrow almost hitting you was panning from aft to stern. If we are lucky, the photographer might have captured the assassin up on the helipad. They might not even know they have it because they are focussing on the arrow strike."

"I see." The prime minister turned his attention back to the ocean and was silent for a moment, perhaps now also a little embarrassed about how he reacted. "I'm afraid I don't know who filmed the incident. It was my assumption that they caught the event through blind luck. I will, however, ask the reporters when I next see them."

"Time is a crucial factor, Radovan. I will go to them when I leave here." I didn't know their names, or which cabins they were staying in, but finding that information wouldn't take long. My visit was at his request, though I, of course, needed to see him anyway, but he was yet to identify why he asked to see me unless it was for nothing more than to ask how the case was progressing.

When I questioned him, he said, "Yes, the case, but also because I wish to host a lunch and cocktail party today. I made some discreet enquiries about the young woman who caught the arrow intended for me. I believe she is now out of medical care, and I would like to formerly apologise. Doing so over lunch is appropriate."

Reading between the lines, I guessed this was another opportunity to get his face in the papers and drive home the attempted assassination story.

However, the lunch would mean I could control his movements for at least part of the day and give me a chance to learn more about Stephanie, so I asked, "How can I help with that?"

"I'm afraid I don't know her name. I tasked my bodyguard with finding out, but the medical staff were very tight-lipped about her personal information. Would you be kind enough to extend the invitation and join us. I spoke with the captain already. The venue is the top deck banquet room. He has assembled a list of attendees."

I couldn't say that spending social time with the prime minister appealed, but this was work. I could also load the area with security officers in plain clothes and hope the assassin was brazen enough to try again. Ok, so I was willing to use a head of nation as bait. We're at sea. The rules are different here.

Missing Something

When we left the suite, I took the dogs from Jermaine, but I paid them and everything around me almost no attention because my mind was elsewhere. Operating on autopilot, I mumbled to Martin that I would meet him and the others in the nest and found myself outside on the deck.

The sun shone down and the warmth of the day blessed my skin despite a gentle breeze. We would arrive in Honolulu later this afternoon, which was good news for Stephanie, provided we could find her husband and eject him, but bad news for the prime minister. He would want to disembark the ship, as was his right, but once ashore he would have almost no protection at all.

His one security guard might be the best in the world, but against a sniper's bullet he would be as effective as wet tissue. You might point out that getting killed off the ship made it not my problem, but that's hardly an attitude I should willingly embrace.

So the clock was ticking. That's how it felt, and I was missing something. I just didn't know what it was and my stroll around the deck was a feeble attempt to give my brain time to consider the equation.

Something about Dale Morris being on the list of possibles for the assassin bothered me. It triggered the familiar itchy skull sensation I always get when I am seeing something significant. But why would he be the assassin? He was here for his wife, going out of his way to continue making her life a misery. When I finally caught up to him, I hoped Jermaine was around to stop me swinging something heavy at his head.

I pushed my brain to think in non-logical lines, but could find no reason why Dale Morris would want to hurt the head of a small European nation. In fact, I was willing to bet he'd never even heard of Radovan Filipovic or Molovia.

"Good morning," said a familiar voice that broke through my concentration.

Looking to my left, I saw Justin Masters, the older gentleman with the Chelsea accent.

"Hello, Justin. Out for another stroll?"

"Indeed. Getting myself some of the good, clean ocean air. I must say I'll be glad to dock in Hawaii. I'm finding life on the ship a little monotonous."

The poor chap. I was all by myself when I first came on board but had the benefit of Jermaine for company even then. Plus I soon made friends, but I hadn't thought about what it must be like for an older person travelling alone.

An idea found its way to my lips. "Would you like to come to a cocktail party? It's happening at one o'clock. I'm going with a couple of lady friends and we could do with a dapper gentleman to escort us."

He grinned cheekily. "Well, I can hardly turn you down now, can I?"

"Wonderful. I have some work to do right now, but I'll come by your suite to collect you just before one. Is that okay?"

"Formal wear, yes?"

"You have a dinner jacket with you?" Most men bring one on a cruise.

"Indeed I do, dear lady. Well, I shall not detain you. Thank you very much for the invitation."

I touched his arm as I walked away, imparting good will to a man I believed would become a friend while he was on board. Justin possessed a certain 'lost soul' vibe that I knew I wouldn't be able to resist.

Ten minutes later I led the dogs toward a door to get back inside the ship. Jermaine, my silent sentinel, got to the door first and held it open.

"To the nest, Madam?"

I replied with a nod, my mind still trying to glimpse a truth that hid just out of sight. Only when we arrived at my team's room did I let it go, and that was mostly because I spotted Sam.

He looked happy, and a naughty voice inside my head had a good idea why.

"Ensign Chalk."

He spun around to face me, his goofy grin beaming. "Yes, Mrs Fisher?"

"A little bird told me that you have a girlfriend."

His grin widened another inch. If he smiled any harder the corners of his mouth would touch his ears.

"Her name is Christina. She has big boobies."

A laugh jumped from my mouth and I had to hide my face. It wasn't just me, though. Schneider, Anders, and Martin were all cracking up. Deepa and Molly were more inclined to roll their eyes, but even they could see it was funny.

In his thirties, I was willing to bet money Sam was still a virgin, but the concept of sex hadn't eluded him.

Squashing my mirth, I said, "Can you tell me anything else about her?"

Sam's eyes rolled up and to the left as he engaged his memory, and I worried for a moment that the young lady's breasts were the only thing he'd taken notice of. Thankfully, I was wrong.

"She's from England, Mrs Fisher. She lives in Sussex which she said is not that far from where my mum and dad live in Kent."

"That's right. It's not far."

Sam continued to grin. "She has brown hair and brown eyes and she works in a theatre as a stage hand but she does some acting as well."

"Well, that's lovely. Is she travelling with anyone?"

"Her mum and dad. They have a cabin on deck fourteen. Their names are Ron and Rose, but I call them Mr and Mrs Appletree. Because that's their name," he added in case we couldn't figure that out for ourselves.

I had a lot of things on my to-do list, but Sam was as close to having a child as I had ever come. If he was in his first proper relationship the other stuff could wait a couple of minutes.

I let the dogs off their leads so they could wander and went to Sam where I pulled him into a hug.

"How did the two of you meet?"

"She came up to me when I was going to bingo with gran and her friends last week."

"Last week?" And I was just finding out now.

"I have seen her every day since. Christina's mum and dad go out a lot to shows and stuff, which means we get to hang out in her cabin."

I chewed on my lips, debating how to pose the question that had just screamed to the front of my mental queue.

Looking Sam straight in the eye, I asked, "Are you being safe?"

"Safe? Um, we keep the door locked and we don't answer it unless it's her mum and dad coming back."

"That's not really what I meant."

Sam's innocent face told me he had no clue what subject I was currently dancing around.

Schneider coughed quietly to get my attention. "I was planning to have a little chat with him later."

Relieved, I let it drop and gave Sam another hug. "I'm very happy for you." When I let him go, I clapped my hands together. It ended the moment and moved me forward. "Now, I could talk about Sam's new girlfriend all day, but work must prevail. Where are we with our forty-seven potential suspects and the search for Dale Morris?"

Team Meeting

It wasn't all bad news, but there wasn't a whole lot of good either. They had reduced the list by half, but we were still looking at twenty-five people. The men, all Caucasian, were roughly the same height, roughly the same age, they were broad across the shoulders and had short hair.

Some of them were married and had their families with them. I wanted to eliminate them as potential suspects simply because they were on board with children, but I could not. There was no reason to believe that a professional assassin would not bring actors along and carry fake passports convincing enough to fool even a trained eye. With that in mind, we were viewing them all as potentials for the assassin. Though I worried we might have it completely wrong still simply because we were, of course, basing everything on the testimony of a single eyewitness who, by his own admission, saw the person who dropped the dumbbell only for the briefest of moments.

The person who filmed the first assassination attempt had still not come forward, and I could see no other way of obtaining their name. I doubted very much that any of the news channels showing the footage would give up their information. The press can be funny like that with the confidentiality of their sources.

PRIME SHOT

Likewise, we had no idea who shot footage of the dumbbell almost hitting the Prime Minister. Yet, just like with the first attempt, this short piece of film had quickly made its way to the news channels.

"We can put the message out again," suggested Deepa. "We might get lucky a second time."

"Should we offer a reward?" asked Molly. "They were clearly motivated by money if they sold it to the news channels." She made a valid point. But I had a sneaking suspicion that they were never going to come forward.

In fact, an idea was forming in my skull, and I was going to have to find some time to focus on it. When I discussed the source of the footage with the prime minister, he acted as though unaware I requested it to the entire ship and embedded a message on the TV in every cabin. There had to be a reason why and I didn't like where my thoughts were leading me.

Despite that, I said, "Good idea, Molly. Let's try it. Can I leave you to set that up, Martin?"

Martin dipped his head. "Absolutely."

The team had cross-referenced the remaining men on the list against the upper deck gym from which the dumbbell had been taken. There is a camera fitted in the gym's reception, and by cross-referencing it with their photographs, they had been able to confirm that not one of the men had stepped foot inside it. Of course, that didn't make them innocent. It merely suggested the inclusion of an accomplice, or even accomplices.

On the far wall, an interactive digital board summed up our thoughts on the case, our list of suspects, and what evidence we'd been able to collate thus far. Unfortunately, there wasn't really very much to record. We had no fingerprints.

We had no physical evidence. We didn't really have any suspects, apart from a list of passengers who matched the description Shane Toomey gave us.

"The ship needs more cameras," said Martin, raising an argument we'd all heard before.

His wife said, "We can't put cameras everywhere, darling."

"We probably could," he countered, "and it would soon cut down on petty crime."

"But this isn't petty crime," said Schneider, "and even with a CCTV camera, we probably wouldn't have been able to catch the guy's face. The witness said he was wearing a hood."

Not to be dissuaded, Martin continued to argue, "Yes, but cameras everywhere would have meant that we caught him somewhere else, unless he kept his hood up and his face hidden all the way to somewhere where there wasn't a camera and then changed to make sure we didn't see him coming out wearing the same outfit. That would require a detailed knowledge of the ship and, might I suggest, a great deal of luck."

I huffed out a sigh and tore my eyes away from the board. "OK, team, I think we can all acknowledge that we're not really getting anywhere with our assassin at this time." It was time to tell them about the Prime Minister's lunch. "It's in just a few hours," I explained. "The captain will be there along with about two hundred guests, and I'm fairly sure Prime Minister Filipovic will ensure the press are there to record it all. It's hard to say whether the assassin might make another attempt at any point, let alone during an unscheduled luncheon/cocktail party thing, but I don't think the Prime Minister announced his plans to have dinner at Frank's French restaurant last night either.

"So whoever it is, they must be watching him closely?" concluded Molly.

"That would be my assumption," I replied.

"I think it unlikely they will strike at lunch. The previous two attempts were in the open. However, we need to be wary. All the while he is on the ship, the Prime Minister is our responsibility. We need to request additional manpower to cover the event. It's not going to be a big or lavish affair, but that doesn't mean that he won't be vulnerable."

With my team listening, I outlined timings, the location, and what I thought we needed to do. I wanted them all in plain clothes. There would be enough of Commander Jandl's security team on show in uniform, so my people would be invisible, mingling with the attendees and keeping an ever-watchful eye for anyone who might be paying the Prime Minister just a little bit too much attention.

With lunch just a few hours away, we needed to get moving if we were going to be ready, especially since I needed to engage Commander Jandl and borrow some of his officers. I delegated that task to Martin and allowed him to depart so he could make the request in person.

Moving down my list, the next task was to visit Stephanie. If she was coming to the lunch, she would want at least a little warning to make herself more presentable, and I wondered if she had something appropriate to wear. If she didn't, that could be my treat, and I'd be more than happy to spend the money. The ship is littered with elegant boutiques. Before that, though, I wanted an update on the search for her husband.

Deepa sounded frustrated and unnecessarily guilty when she reported they'd been equally ineffective in locating him as they had in identifying the assassin.

"He hasn't been back to his cabin. We know that much," she said.

"There was a full sweep of the ship last night when we were trying to find Stephanie," said Anders. "All the security officers and crew have his photograph. He won't even be able to get any food without somebody spotting him."

"So it should just be a matter of time," I concluded. "He'll show up somewhere, and then we have him."

"What's the plan when we do identify him?" Deepa wanted to know.

I'd been giving this some thought. "I think there's a little bit of grey area where I'm going to play around. Rest assured though, Dale Morris is going to the brig. He's not getting to his wife, that's for certain. If he complains, what's the worst that can happen? Someone senior at Purple Star will shout at me. I'll take that on the chin. But he *is* guilty of assaulting her. I've seen her wounds, and his presence on this ship falls into the category of stalking. She didn't know that he was on board, and they are staying in separate cabins."

"He'll argue coincidence and claim he was just on a cruise," Deepa argued.

"Yes, he probably will and that's why someone will end up shouting at me. I don't care. This is about Stephanie. She's on the run, so for her safety, even if it costs me my job, which I very much doubt it will, I am going to lock him up. It's only going to be for a few hours."

"Yes," said Schneider, "we should be pulling into Honolulu in eight hours. What if we haven't found him by then?"

"Then he will either attempt to get off, in which case we've got him, or he'll stay on the ship. And with the majority of the passengers no longer on it, we'll be able to scour it deck by deck." I didn't have to say that this would mean all of them and a chunk of the crew would have their shore leave cancelled until he was found. My team all knew it and were professional enough to accept it as part of the job. I couldn't say that I was excited to stay on board instead of going ashore in Hawaii either, but unless Dale Morris had jumped overboard, he was still somewhere on board the Aurelia, and he would be found.

I would hand him over to Honolulu PD and make a big noise about his stalking. They wouldn't have anything to charge him with, but I believed that I could scare him enough that he would get the message. He wasn't getting to Stephanie, and she now had friends who would not only protect her but would pay for a legal team to drive his face into the dirt.

All points covered, for now at least, I announced that I was going to leave them to get on with it.

"What about that necklace?" asked Molly. "The one that came from the jewellery heist."

"Well, it needs to be returned to the jewellers. That would be stage one. But you're right to bring it up, because its presence on the ship suggests that the thief is here too."

"Thief?" questioned Deepa. "It was a jewellery heist. We can't be talking about one person. They broke into a vault."

"Yes. I find it all a little concerning. But right now, we have more pressing matters. The crime was not committed on the Aurelia, and I am the ship's detective. So, with assassins and stalkers to worry about... this will get my attention later."

I called for my dogs to let them know that we were leaving, clipped them back to their leads, and went to find Stephanie Morris.

Skill Set

"Lunch with a prime minister?" Stephanie sounded distinctly unsure. "I don't know, Patricia. I don't know anything about politics. He's going to want to talk to me and I'm going to have nothing intelligent to say."

I did my best to reassure her. "No one is going to make you attend, Stephanie. If you don't want to go, you have the right to refuse."

She looked doubtful. "That's going to come across as rude, though, isn't it?"

"Not necessarily." I was trying to reassure her but knew it hadn't come out as convincing as I intended.

As per my instructions, Stephanie had been moved to a new cabin. The replacement was on deck fourteen and right next to one of the security team crew rooms. If she screamed for help, it would arrive within seconds.

Anna and Georgie were exploring, snuffling round the carpet looking for crumbs of food and poking their noses under the edge of the bed. They would get bored of their exploration after a little while and most likely find a soft piece of carpet on which to settle down for a snooze.

I had no opinion regarding whether Stephanie should attend the luncheon or not. However, I doubted Prime Minister Filipovic would ask her any taxing questions. Perhaps I was being overly harsh, but I felt it likely his only reason for inviting her was another photo opportunity, a chance to string out the failed assassination attempts just a little longer.

Nevertheless, I said, "Lunch will give you the chance to meet the captain. And an opportunity for you and I to discuss what is going to happen next. I expect the food will be nice too."

"Patricia," Stephanie drew the word out, making me think she had something she wasn't quite sure how to ask, "you haven't said anything about my husband. Am I to take it that this means he hasn't been found yet?"

I probably should have started with the news, but I knew I had nothing good to tell her.

"Yes, that is the case. It's just a matter of time before we find him, though. The entire crew have seen his photograph and those with tablets have a copy of it. He won't be able to get off the ship in Honolulu without us catching him. Honestly, I don't think you should worry too much about him now. He has no freedom of movement, so he won't be trying to get to you. I believe he has gone to ground to avoid getting caught. Catching up to you will be the last thing on his mind."

I genuinely believed what I was saying was true. That he was proving so hard to find and had not returned to his cabin had to mean all his effort was focused on avoiding the ship's security officers.

"Oh, Dale, where are you?" Stephanie sighed. Her eyes were down, staring at nothing much, so I gave her a few seconds to dwell on her thoughts before interrupting them.

"Lunch?" I prompted. "As I said before, no one is going to make you go, but it would not do any harm to get out and mingle." When she looked up at me, I showed her a wide grin. "It's also a chance to dress up a little fancy. How about if I take you shopping at one of my favourite boutiques. My treat."

She was going to protest, so like a freight train moving at speed, I became unstoppable. Rising from my chair, I called for the dogs, hooked my handbag over my shoulder, and said, "They have the loveliest range of cocktail dresses. I'll have my good friend Barbie meet us there and all three of us can get something new. Barbie is always a hit at these events."

A ripple of mirth crossed Jermaine's face before he wrestled it back under control. We both knew why my blonde friend was always so warmly received at formal events, or indeed anywhere for that matter. She is stunningly attractive, and there isn't a dress in the world that can hide her assets.

It was mid-morning, so on our way to the boutique on deck eighteen, I stopped with Stephanie to get coffee and pastries. I needed to kill time until Barbie could join us, plus slowing the pace of our day provided a perfect opportunity to pick her brains about potential future employment on board the ship.

"I don't really know what I have to offer. Dale never wanted me to have a job. He was always so jealous. He never said it, but I think he wanted to avoid me meeting other men, which I would have with almost any job."

"Were you employed before you married him?"

"Yes, we only got married three years ago. I guess I wasn't very career driven. I worked in a couple of fast-food chains when I was a teenager, then retail jobs as a shop assistant. But I don't have what anyone would call 'skills'."

"How about school? Do you have any qualifications that might help me to find you something appropriate. This ship is a lot like a floating city. Almost any job you might find in the city can be found here too."

"Well, I can drive a car." Stephanie pulled a face to show she was making a joke, then dropped the smile to make it clear she had something serious to say. "Patricia, I honestly don't mind what I end up doing. You're being so generous with your time. You have cleaners on board and that is one skill I can claim. If they have vacancies there, that will do me."

I wanted to push her, not because there was anything wrong with being a cleaner. Far from it. I used to be a cleaner. But it was one of the lower paying roles, and I knew that money was an issue for her. She was starting her life again in her early thirties and without a penny to her name. Finding her a job that paid more would only serve to help. I made a mental note to research her academic qualifications and employment record later. I would be prying, no doubt about it, but doing so with the best of intentions.

She looked embarrassed by the conversation so I dropped it and started talking about the Aurelia and all the places that she would visit in just the next few weeks if she remained on board.

"It's so exotic," she said, her eyes alight with the possibility of life on board a luxury cruise ship. "It's already so different from anything I've experienced in my life."

"You did a very brave thing, Stephanie. Now you get to reap the reward for your courage."

"Hey, Patty!" Barbie called as she came into the coffee shop.

Stephanie caught sight of her and I got to watch her eyes bug from her head.

"Wow! Are those things real?"

I sighed. "Yup. Annoying, isn't she?"

Barbie sashayed through the room with almost all eyes following her path. Clad in a lycra sports bra and a pair of booty shorts, the form fitting material showed off her perfect figure and toned body. I could see every one of her abdominal muscles. In my opinion, a woman with so little body fat should not be able to sport gravity defying double D breasts. Yet there she was, chest bouncing.

"Hey there. You must be Stephanie. Patty has been telling me all about you. Are you going to be joining the crew?"

Stephanie shrugged which caused her to wince. The injury to her shoulder would take some time to heal.

"It's starting to look that way," she said. "Have you worked on the ship for long?"

Barbie grabbed a chair from a nearby unoccupied table and sat down to join us.

"Long enough to know that I don't want to do anything else anytime soon. I don't think there's any better way to see the world."

Barbie knew better than to ask questions about the poor woman's husband and the awful situation she found herself in. There would be time for that if she got to know her better. For now, we were going shopping.

Except we never got there.

Closing the Net

Leaving the coffee shop on deck nineteen, I sent Jermaine back to my suite with the dogs. They'd had a decent amount of exercise and a boutique selling designer apparel was not the right place for them. It was only a short hop to get to the escalators that would take us down to the next deck where the bulk of the ship's shopping outlets could be found, but riding it down, I was standing behind Stephanie when she spasmed in shock.

Her uninjured arm shot out like an arrow and she shouted, "Dale!"

Sure enough, on the up escalator just four feet to our right, a broad-shouldered man wearing a hoodie and a ball cap snapped his head up to reveal his face.

Dale's mouth hung open, his shock apparent, but only for a split second. Before I had a chance to react, he barged through the couple in front and raced up the stairs. I scrambled to get hold of my radio and turned around. I needed to fight my way back up the escalator even as it was descending.

Barbie being Barbie chose a more direct route. With one hand on the rail, she vaulted off the down escalator, performed a handstand on the sloping surface in between, and dropped onto the up escalator, her arms and legs already pumping to give chase.

She did so amid gasps of surprise from everyone in sight, but what shocked me most was seeing Stephanie follow. It must have hurt to use her right arm, and I heard a grunt of pain, but she clambered up, out, and across the centre divide to also give chase.

Yelling into the radio, I gave my location and called for any security officers in the vicinity to come. Before I could finish squawking for help, the blonde gym instructor had reached the top of the escalator and vanished from sight.

Releasing my radios send switch, I shouted, "Stephanie! What do you think you're doing?" She was slower than Barbie, but so is almost everyone else on the planet and Barbie didn't have an injury to slow her down. Whether powered by a moment of madness or simply desperate to ensure her vile husband would be apprehended, she also reached the top of the up escalator and vanished from sight.

I needed to get after them and my attempt to fight my way back up the down escalator had thus far resulted in getting me absolutely nowhere.

Knowing Barbie, I expected to find Dale Morris lying on his stomach, pinned to the floor with Barbie's knee between his shoulder blades. He's a big man, but she is fast, she is strong, and she is fierce.

I had to get there quick.

I was two-thirds of the way down now, but left in the dust of younger women, I sensed that it was time to show I still had what it took. Mirroring their moves and with the radio now in my left hand, I grabbed hold of the escalator's rubber rail and vaulted up onto the sloping central divide.

PRIME SHOT

I wasn't about to perform a handstand, like Barbie, but Stephanie had scrambled across it like a mountain goat on a cliff face. She made it look easy enough that I thought I would be able to do much the same.

I was wrong.

The moment I tried to grip the metal surface with my shoes I discovered it had all the friction qualities of a sheet of ice. In full view of the people on both sides of the escalator, and all those filling the atrium below, plus those now hanging over the railings on the deck above, my feet went out from under me.

Landing on my belly, I scratched and clawed for any kind of grip, found none and for the first time in many, many years, I enjoyed the playground sensation that is a slide.

Although, perhaps 'enjoyed' is not the correct word. I slid the remaining yards to the bottom of the escalator, my dress gathering around my waist, where gravity spat me out into free air, three feet above the ground.

There were perhaps dozens of people who could have arrested my fall by throwing an arm out to stop me. However, they all chose to watch instead.

In what I've come to recognize as typical Patricia's style, I hung in the air for a moment, looking like Jean-Claude Van Damme performing one of his miraculous karate kicks. That description suggests a pose more graceful than I achieved, but needless to say it didn't last long. Without my body pinning my dress to my butt, it ballooned with air, exposing everything south of my neck even though I fought to push it back down. When Marilyn Monroe danced on top of that subway grate, she looked great. I doubted the same could be said for me.

Still fighting my dress, I slammed into the deck with the meat of my bottom leading the way.

Had I stuck with the jeans I picked out first this morning, they would have protected my derriere from the worst of the friction burn, but I went with the dress so I would look cute and now I got to wear it around my head.

I could hear people taking pictures with their phones and swore to the heavens for my choice of underwear. When I last showed the world my knickers, I gained brief notoriety as an internet sensation called 'Granny Pants'. I was doing it again today, only in more spectacular style.

Cursing my luck, I grabbed the hem of my dress, and yanked it back into place as I sat up. All around me, gawping faces filled my field of vision. You could have fried eggs on the heat radiating off my face. Patricia Fisher, the infamous sleuth, once again showing the world her underwear. Hurrah!

A few kindly souls offered to help me back to my feet, but desperate to get back into the hunt for Dale, I rolled onto my front, got my feet under my body, and took off like a sprinter from the blocks.

That lasted about two paces at which point the pain in my backside registered. Grumbling under my breath, I mounted the escalator and limped up it at my best speed.

Radio chatter told me Dale was yet to be found. It defied my expectations. I had fully expected they would have caught him by now. How on earth had he outpaced Barbie? She's like a gazelle.

Winded by the time I got to the top of the escalator, I couldn't see Barbie or Stephanie, or any of the security officers I hoped to find sitting on top of Stephanie's husband. What I did find, however, were the two bounty hunters.

Mason saw me at the same time I saw them. He elbowed Edgar and murmured something I suspected probably wasn't all that charitable, before heading away from me.

I could only guess they were still searching for their fugitive. Their escapades were way down my list of priorities, but as I lifted my radio to get a situation report and find out where everyone was, I heard Commander Jandl's voice come across the airwaves.

"Increase the search radius. Blakely and Alvers go aft. Khan, take four and head to the port side. I'll sweep in from starboard. If he's inside our net, we'll find him."

Alerting commander Jandl to my presence, I said, "This is Mrs Fisher. I'm at the top of the escalators on deck nineteen. There's no sign of him here, over."

Two seconds later, the commander's voice returned, "Please stay where you are, Mrs Fisher. I'm going to send someone to you just in case he doubles back."

I did as requested, my eyes alert for any sign of Dale Morris. If he came this way, if I saw a shadow I thought could be his, I would holler into the microphone to bring the security officers in my direction and do whatever it took to stop him from escaping. He wasn't here, though, and less than a minute later, two white uniforms emerged from a side passageway at a jog.

Recognising Delany and Horobin, I raised my arm and waved it to get their attention. They slowed their pace to a walk, their eyes vigilant as they scanned the deck. When they joined me, they didn't ask if I'd seen any sign of Dale, they simply turned their attention outwards, and listened to the chatter coming over the radio.

Five minutes passed, and with each one our hope of catching him diminished. Increasingly frustrated, I could feel my jaw muscles beginning to ache. I was clenching my teeth again. The search was not going well, which is to say it was already obvious that he had slipped away or found somewhere to hide. Commander Jandl was being thorough, but we were not going to catch Dale Morris this time.

I heard him give the call to stand everyone down just as I spotted Stephanie returning. She looked angry, but whatever emotion clouded her mind, all I felt was relief. She didn't have a radio, and I hadn't gotten around to taking her phone number, so I had no idea where she was, and the paranoid part of my brain worried her absence meant Dale had grabbed her.

I left Delany and Horobin to check on her.

"Are you okay?"

Still looking annoyed, Stephanie gave a stiff shake of her head. "Yes, I'm fine. I just can't believe he was right there."

"What were you thinking?" It was a question I'd shouted at her back when she first chased after her husband. "What would you have done if you caught up to him?"

"I don't know," she admitted sheepishly. "Probably screamed for help, I guess. I just saw him, and I was so angry that he followed me here. He believes that marriage is for life, and that the only way out of it is for one of us to die."

It horrified me to know that there were men out there who thought like that.

A voice behind me said, "Mrs Fisher?" And I turned to find Commander Jandl looking down at me. The tall South African man stands well over six feet tall, but it is his muscle that makes him such an imposing figure. I can't say that I've ever been particularly impressed by bodybuilders. Stretching and inflating their frames to such unnatural proportions all seems a bit extreme to me, yet I suppose there are far worse hobbies a person could pursue.

Though I knew the question was pointless, I asked, "No luck?"

"I'm afraid not, Mrs Fisher. He gave us the slip this time. I have called the search off and have stood the teams down. They are returned to their posts, but will continue to look out for him. Is this Mrs Morris?" He switched his attention to Stephanie.

"Yes," she said. "If your men do spot him, it's okay by me if they accidentally shoot him a few times. But I would appreciate it if they didn't kill him straight away. There are a few things I would like to say while I have the chance."

Commander Jandl's face searched for a suitable expression. Was she being serious? Was this an appropriate time to laugh? Unable to decide, he escaped the situation by calling to one of his subordinates and leaving us as though he had something urgent to which he must attend.

His departure left me alone with Stephanie.

"Shall we see about those dresses now?" I suggested, thinking it was a good time to distract her with some retail therapy.

She sagged a little, and offering me an apologetic face, said, "I'm really not in the mood anymore. Sorry, Patricia. I think I'd like to go back to my cabin now. I have something I can wear to a cocktail party. It's not new, but it will do."

I thought about trying to persuade her, but decided against it. A check of my watch showed that I had just under two hours until it was time for our lunch appointment with Prime Minister Filipovic. More than enough to get myself ready, which meant I could squeeze in some research. I would start with Stephanie. I still believed there would be a better paid job than cleaning if I could just figure out where her skills lay.

"Come along then. I'll walk you back to your cabin. I want to make sure you get there okay."

"That's really not necessary," Stephanie began to say, but I gave her no choice. I'd just seen for myself, the size difference between her and Dale. If he caught up to her, he could snap her neck like a twig.

Barbie found us just as we were leaving the deck nineteen shopping area. I wanted to ask her how Stephanie's husband had managed to give her the slip, but she began to explain almost before she reached me.

"I almost ran into a stroller. There was just no way around it, and I couldn't leap it because there were people on the other side. It slowed me down enough that he slipped into one of the side passageways and I never saw him again after that. He's fast, too. Was he a track athlete?"

Stephanie fielded the question that was obviously aimed at her. "A wide receiver. He used to be able to cover a hundred metres in under eleven seconds."

Barbie gave a low whistle. "Then he would have been hard to catch."

"And I once thought he was a catch." Stephanie's final comment killed the conversation, and we walked the rest of the way to her cabin in silence.

Time to Die

Barbie and I left Stephanie at her new cabin and were walking back to my suite when she asked about the ongoing cases. I hadn't seen her since yesterday, and she had questions about the necklace, the hunt for the assassin, and my plans for Stephanie.

Since I met the young woman from California on my second day on board, she had acted as a sounding board for my thoughts and ideas as well as a life coach in some respects. Despite her tender age of just twenty-two, Barbie had her life organised way better than I'd ever managed.

Exiting the elevator and shocked Barbie hadn't forced me to take the stairs for once – she was all for cramming in a little unplanned exercise – we arrived on the top deck to find our way blocked.

The passageway leading directly to my suite had barrier tape strewn haphazardly across it and yellow fold out signs warning of a slip hazard. But there was no sign of anyone trying to clean it up and I couldn't see a spill anywhere.

"Maybe someone was sick," Barbie guessed. "Whoever found it first would have roped it off to keep people back and gone to fetch the gear to deal with it."

Whatever the case, it wouldn't do to just ignore the barrier, so we took the long route. Specifically, the long route meant backtracking a little bit along the top deck to the nearest set of doors. Using them, we accessed the outer deck. It added at least a hundred yards to our journey, but that wasn't exactly a big deal, and it was pleasant and sunny outside. Squinting into the distance as we walked towards the bow, I questioned whether I could see Hawaii.

"Would it be visible yet?" I asked Barbie.

Prompted by my question, Barbie cupped her hands around her eyes and squinted into the distance, then used her right arm to point.

"I think that blob on the horizon is Big Island."

This was only my second trip to the Hawaiian Islands, and I was very excited to return there. I just hoped I could wrap up my current cases and be able to spend my fully allotted amount of time ashore. We were about halfway between the two sets of doors when I heard a kind of twanging noise from above us. It pulled my eyes around to see where it had come from, but there was nothing I could see that could have made it. That changed a heartbeat later when one of the lifeboats shifted.

And when I say shifted, what I mean is one end of the entire lifeboat fell free from its moorings. Where it was anchored at the lifeboat's stern, it remained in place, which left the rest of it to pivot about that point.

My feet froze, and my brain told me I was about to die. The ship's lifeboats are not what one could call small or light items. Mounted all along the sides of the ship's superstructure, they are operated with hydraulic cranes that manoeuvre them out over the edge and then down into the water. This one wasn't going to make it to the water. It was going to swing right through the spot where I stood. I knew that I needed to run, but at the same time, I could already calculate that doing so wouldn't help. There was altogether too much lifeboat, moving way too fast for me to avoid.

Thankfully, as I may have mentioned before, Barbie moves rather more quickly than most people. I heard her yell something, but whatever it was got drowned out in the fog of my terrified brain. The next thing I knew, she had lifted me bodily from the deck and I was being thrown out of the way. Idly, as I felt gravity snatch me from the air, I wondered if this was what it felt like to play rugby.

Completely out of control, I hit the deck with a crunch, leading with my bottom, which was quite sore enough from my previous fall, thank you very much. Unable to fight the momentum, the back of my head smacked into the unyielding deck too, bringing stars to my eyes and a taste of blood to my mouth. My vision swirled, though only for half a second, and it just so happened that my eyes were looking up at the lifeboat mounting point at the right time to see a figure looking back down at me.

The distance was too great to make out any features, but it was clearly a man, and he looked to be broad-shouldered. Hidden inside a hoodie, I couldn't see his face, just like Dale Morris's had been. And my heart thumped as I questioned if the man I had just seen could have been Stephanie's husband. He was only there for a fleeting moment, ducking out of the way the moment he saw my eyes swing in his direction.

Barbie rolled off me and swung her legs around to get them back beneath her body. In one lithe movement, she was back on her feet and looking around for any further signs of danger.

"Whoo, that was close," she said. "Patty, are you okay?"

She reached down to offer me a hand up. I took it, thankful for her help.

"You saved me," I pointed out.

She shrugged. "I could hardly let you get crushed."

The lifeboat now hung drunkenly from its rear mounting point. Looking up I could see the mechanism was now bent, the weight pulling it in a direction it was not designed to go. People were coming, their cries of surprise and excited chatter drawing even more to investigate. Many were in bathing suits, a whole raft of them coming from the deck's main sun terrace. Mums and dads, grannies and grandpas, kids and all, their morbid curiosity demanding they see what had happened. Members of the crew came running too, forcing their way through the passengers and politely insisting they stay back.

Now back on my feet, I walked over to the lifeboat. A member of the crew said, "Please stay back, Mrs Fisher. That might not be safe. I'll get engineering up here."

His advice was probably sound, but I wanted to know why the lifeboat had fallen. I didn't think it was an accident. Not for one minute. A theory that was proven the moment I got a proper look at the lifeboat's anchor point. Barbie saw it too.

"Someone undid the bolts," she gasped. "Oh, my goodness, this was deliberate."

"Barbie, when you tackled me, I spotted someone, and I think it was Dale Morris."

"Stephanie's husband?"

I told her about the man I saw. The area above the top deck is reserved for crew only, and yet again, someone had managed to get up there. Possibly they were crew, but the itch at the back of my skull told me that probably wasn't the case. All the while I explained things to her, I was fumbling for my phone. My hands were shaking from the sudden burst of adrenaline, but I clenched my fists, forced my fingers to obey my commands and started to talk.

"Martin, this is Patricia. Someone just tried to kill me. I need all of you to be aware Dale Morris is going on the offensive against us."

"It was Dale Morris?"

Was it?

"I think so, yes. No ... I can't be sure. It looked a lot like him, but it was too far away to be sure. My point is that if he believes we are trying to stop him from getting to his wife, he might have chosen to be proactive in tackling us first. I want you to brief the team and make sure they are extra vigilant."

"I will do that. You're not hurt though, right?"

"Just shaken. He tried to drop a lifeboat on me."

"That was you? I just heard about that over the radio. Commander Jandl just sent half the security officers on duty to deal with it."

The sound of boots on the deck told me they were arriving at speed.

"I've got to go. They will want to speak with me." I ended the call in time to see Commander Jandl exiting the ship's superstructure.

"In the thick of it again?" he observed.

"Aren't I always?" I shot back with a sad laugh.

I didn't point out the missing anchor bolts and he found them almost immediately, his eyebrows rising to show his surprise.

"I'd better call the captain," he said.

"I think it better if you inform Commander Ochi. The captain has a lunch date in just over an hour. The deputy captain can update him when he has the chance."

I got a nod, but no verbal response.

The security officers had the onlookers under control and the lifeboat was no longer of any interest to me. The attempt on my life and the person who perpetrated it were.

"Commander, it is almost certainly too late already, but you should seal off the helideck."

"I already did that, Mrs Fisher, and I have officers searching it now. Unfortunately, there are many ways to get down to the top deck and I suspect they will have escaped again."

"Again?"

"Is this not the same assassin who missed Prime Minister Filipovic yesterday? He will know you are closing in by now."

Questions swirled around my head. Was it the assassin? Was it Dale Morris? Could it be a third party?

The radios crackled and a voice said, "Commander Jandl, we've found a rope. Looks like whoever it was used it to get up and down. They fashioned a grappling hook using duct tape and cutlery and threw it over the railing to get around the locked doors.

"A grappling hook?" I questioned.

Commander Jandl had his radio halfway to his mouth when he said, "You can fix anything with duct tape."

Whoever I saw had made good their escape, so I left the head of the security team to manage his subordinates and wandered back to Barbie.

PRIME SHOT

"Are we still doing the lunch?" she asked.

In the excitement, I'd forgotten all about it.

Airtag

No one else tried to kill me or Barbie or anyone else in the short walk from the stricken lifeboat to my suite. The security team confirmed the spill signs and taped off passageway were fake, a diversion to send me into the path of the boobytrap. The most worrying part of that realisation was the need to acknowledge they knew where I was, where I was going, and where to set a trap.

I didn't know how, and that was scaring me.

Arriving back at my cabin, I found Lady Mary sitting at the breakfast bar with a gin and tonic. I checked my watch to confirm it was after noon, not that the time of day seemed to make much difference to her. She would drink Buck's fizz or a Bloody Mary for breakfast most days.

Handing my jacket to Jermaine, I called, "Good afternoon, Mary."

"It is now," she raised her glass in a toast. "Have you been working again? Isn't it a little early to be catching criminals?"

I fussed the dogs, who are always excited to see me even when we have only been apart for a short while, and joined her in the kitchen.

PRIME SHOT

"Some tea, Madam?"

"Tea would be lovely, thank you, sweetie." To answer Lady Mary, I said, "Unfortunately, it is never too early for criminals, though I'm not sure quite how to label Dale Morris."

"That's the wife beater?"

"Yes."

She picked up her drink. "There'll be no need for a label if you simply toss him overboard."

I worried she might do it if our roles were reversed.

Barbie still had some of her dresses in the wardrobe in what today was Lady Mary's room. I thought she accompanied me to the suite so she could fetch one, but it turned out that wasn't her only reason.

"Patty nearly got killed," she told Jermaine.

The glass in his right hand smashed as he crushed it with his hand.

"I'm fine, sweetie," I assured him while shooting daggers at Barbie.

She held her hands up in surrender, but said, "I'm not going to get involved, but his talents are wasted making cocktails. He's part ninja and has the reflexes of a cat. You need him next to you, Patty. That lifeboat almost squished you."

I sighed and dropped myself down onto a barstool.

"Someone undid the bolts anchor the mount at one end. It swung through the air and Barbie had to throw me out of its path."

Barbie tried to play her heroics down. "Anyone else would have done the same. You would have saved her, wouldn't you, Lady Mary?"

Lady Mary pursed her lips. "Am I holding one gin or two in this scenario?"

Dismissing her response, I slipped off the barstool again. "I need to get ready and so do you, Blondie. We have lunch in forty minutes, and I still need to collect Stephanie and Justin."

Barbie cocked an eyebrow. "Justin?"

I explained about our escort for the party.

"He sounds very sweet," Barbie concluded.

Turning to go, I tried to hook my handbag, but knocked it over, spilling some of the contents. My phone, a pack of latex gloves, my hairbrush with spare hairbands around the handle … and a small disc.

Squinting my eyes, I peered at it.

"What's the Airtag for?" asked Barbie.

I chewed my lip and voiced the only answer I had. "For tracking my location."

Jermaine came closer.

Reaching out with my right hand, I picked the small disc up. It weighed no more than a couple of ounces.

Barbie and Lady Mary crowded in next to me.

Lady Mary asked, "You think someone put that in your handbag so they would know where you were?"

I nodded. "I think that is how they knew when to undo the final bolt holding the lifeboat in place. Whoever put this in my bag, and I have a good idea who it was, wanted to know when to close off the passageway that diverted us outside. They tried to kill me. The question is why."

"So who was it, Patty?" Barbie demanded to know.

I refused to say simply because I could be wrong. Basing my suspicion on circumstance and opportunity, what I lacked was any kind of motive. If I was right about the who, I had absolutely no idea why.

Unless ...

"I need to think," I announced, resuming my journey to the bedroom. I had even less time now and I was attending the lunch thing with two younger women.

Naturally, when I returned from my bedroom, now sporting a fire engine red cocktail dress with matching heels and bag, Jermaine was waiting for me. Yet again, he was out of his butler's livery – not that I ever felt he needed to wear it – and resplendent in a killer suit. This one was bright yellow and he wore it with a white shirt and tie, plus white brogues. It wouldn't work on most men, but on my statuesque butler it looked just right.

I nodded appreciatively and accepted his arm to hold. Anna and Georgie ran across the room excited to come with us only to be disappointed this time.

"Sorry, girls. This party is not for doggies." They shot me frowns through the closing door, but I knew they would be contentedly asleep on the couch before I reached the elevators.

At Stephanie's cabin, Jermaine rapped his knuckles firmly on her door and waited. My thoughts were elsewhere, mostly on her husband, in fact, and a worrying concept that refused to leave my mind. Had they not been, it might not have taken me so long to realise the conversation I could hear was coming from behind her door. She was talking to a man. At least I thought she was, and I stiffened.

Had Dale found her? Was he on the other side of the door with a weapon in his hand to control her actions?

Panic tore through me, but when she opened the door a moment later, there was no one visible inside. Stephanie had on a charcoal cocktail dress that showed off her trim figure. A bolero covered her shoulders to hide the sling and the dressing on her shoulder. Once again, I found myself impressed by her resilience.

However, I had to ask, "Sorry, were you with someone?" I glanced past her to look for a tell-tale second coffee mug or glass.

"No. Why would you think that?"

There was no sign that anyone had been with her, but the man's voice …

"I thought I heard someone."

"It was the TV," Stephanie replied, a frown accompanying her dismissive tone as she exited her cabin.

I was still trying to look around her cabin and she almost bumped into me in her haste to get the door shut. There was something she wasn't saying, and my cheeks coloured when I silently questioned if she'd taken a lover. It would explain the man's voice and her wish to hide the truth. And who could blame her for wanting someone who could protect her if Dale did show up?

I let it go and nudged Jermaine to start walking. To cover up my intrusive behaviour, I said, "I hope you are not too hungry. These lunch affairs tend to be a little light on the food."

"But it's lunch?" Stephanie questioned.

"There will be trays of blinis and little canapes, but you have to eat a lot of them to feel full and watch out for the cocktails and champagne. No good meeting the captain and being tipsy when you make your first impression."

"I'll keep that in mind."

Stephanie sounded distracted, like her thoughts were elsewhere, but she was about to meet some of the ship's senior officers and since she was looking for employment on board, this was the perfect chance to impress someone.

"Have you given any more thought to what sort of job you could do? What skills you might be able to offer?"

"Not really. Like I said, anything will do. I don't mind being a cleaner. Or I could work in a bar."

Maybe she was right and that was her pace, but she came across as so capable, so focused.

"How about security?" I tried to sound like I was being casual and not pushing.

"Oh, no. I could never do anything like that. Guns scare me."

Her answers were short, giving me the impression she wanted done with the conversation. I let it die and we walked in silence the rest of the way. She wasn't telling me everything, and some of the things she had told me were not true. At least I didn't think they were, and like so many other things today, it was making my skull itch.

Cocktail Party

We collected Justin last as his suite wasn't far from the banquet room. He was in one of the plusher suites, but not one that came with a butler which meant he really was all alone on the cruise. Seeing that, I resolved to spend more time with him.

A steward announced us as we entered the banquet room set out for the Prime Minister's cocktail lunch. A few heads turned, but the room was already mostly full and the buzz of conversation drowned out the steward's voice. Clinking glasses, polite laughter, and the click of high heels on the wooden deck all added to the background hum.

Barbie hooked her arm through Justin's. "Patty needs to introduce Stephanie to some people. Why don't you come with me and tell me all about where you live. You're English, yes?" I heard her say as she steered him through the crowd.

Looking around I spotted Schneider – easy because he's so tall - then Martin and then Molly. My whole team was here somewhere. In dinner jackets or cocktail dresses, they were mingling as per my advice and keeping their eyes peeled.

"There's the captain," I pointed Alistair out for Stephanie. "He has already agreed to find a place for you among the crew. There are openings in most of the ship's departments. Of course, lots of them require specialist skills, but I know he will be able to offer you work."

"That's good."

I took her short response to be a sign of nerves and hooked my arm through hers for support.

"Come on. You might as well meet him now and get it over with."

"Will I have to meet that Prime Minister guy, too?"

"Probably, but really it's just a photo opportunity for him. And, to be honest, you caught an arrow meant for him. Saying thank you in person is the decent thing for him to do."

Stephanie kept her lips closed, a worried expression on her face, but she let me guide her through the room. Prime Minister Filipovic was to our left, over by the windows facing the prow of the ship. It was a good spot for photographs. I figured I would take Stephanie there next and get it over with so the poor woman could relax.

Alistair saw me coming and broke away from his group to meet me.

"Patricia, darling." He took my hand and kissed it like a gentleman from a bygone era. "And this must be Stephanie." He took her hand too. "I am so terribly sorry that you suffered such a grievous injury on board my ship. I hope you can believe we are doing all we can to bring the archer to justice."

Stephanie reclaimed her hand. "Oh, yes, Patricia is being very thorough. I wouldn't want to be in the assassin's shoes."

"Quite so. Now I have been advised of your situation and that you are keen to secure lodgings and employment on board the Aurelia."

"Is that okay?" Stephanie replied nervously.

"Now is not the time to discuss the subject. However, I would like you to rest assured it is within my power to make that happen. You are scheduled to depart in Honolulu later today, so time is a factor I cannot ignore. To that end, I will send a representative from the bursar's office to speak with you after this party. We can have you set up and in crew accommodation before the end of the day." Alistair shot his eyes at me for approval. "Does that meet with your immediate needs?"

Her cheeks flushing red, Stephanie stammered, "Yes, sir. I mean, captain. I mean .."

Alistair smiled warmly. "You are not crew yet, Mrs Morris. Please call me Alistair."

Commander Lutz appeared behind Alistair and tapped him on the shoulder. Whatever he had to say had to be important, so as Alistair turned to see who was there, I steered Stephanie away.

"Oh, my God. I swear I thought I was going to pass out. Is he allowed to be that handsome?"

A snort of laughter left via my nose.

"Let's get you some champagne. It will take the edge off."

Hearing me, Jermaine swooped on the nearest steward, lifting two flutes from the silver tray she carried with a nod and a smile.

Stephanie downed half the glass with her first sip, tipped her head back and let a shudder shake her body. Bringing her head back to level, she looked distinctly more relaxed.

"Better?"

"Much. Let's go see the Europolitician chap and get that over with. Then maybe I can have another of these and find something to eat."

"You did great with the captain," I told her. We were winding our way through the room to where Prime Minister Filipovic still held centre stage. I doubted he wanted to do anything more than enquire about her injury and wish her a speedy recovery. In public, where he could be seen and heard doing it. It would take no more than a few moments of our time.

However, I heard a radio squawk, and then another. There was something about the insistent noise they made that put me on edge. I guess I tensed because Jermaine was at my side in a heartbeat.

"Madam?"

I looked around, trying to spot someone in uniform. There was a tension in the air that no one around me could sense. The passengers were not reacting if they could, but that aligned with my expectations. My life is fraught with danger so regularly I have learned to listen for its approach.

Spotting Alistair through the crowded room, I changed my trajectory, but stopped before I had gone more than a foot in his direction.

"Jermaine, sweetie, please take Stephanie to meet Prime Minister Filipovic. I will join you shortly." There was a crowd around him, and he wouldn't recognise her without me by her side, so I doubted they would be seen before I had a chance to find out what was going on.

Jermaine's face made it clear he wanted to stay by my side, but I had a feeling I might be needed and wasn't going to drag Stephanie into any more danger. I left him before he could argue.

To the untrained eye, it would probably look as though nothing was happening, but I could see the looks passing between Alistair and a couple of his senior officers. Hushed words gave instructions, the men receiving them then making their way purposefully, if not overtly, toward the banquet room's exit.

"What is it?" I asked, ducking around a steward and their tray to tap Alistair's arm.

"One of the crew has been attacked. A passenger found Ensign Kapur unconscious in a restroom on deck fourteen. His sidearm and uniform are missing."

This was the argument against the ship's security officers carrying sidearms. If there are no guns, no one can hope to get a gun, but the harsh reality is that they need them all too often. Security is tighter now than when I first came on board. Some would say that was due to me and the trouble that seems to follow wherever I go, but it is true that we haven't had an incident with a smuggled gun in months.

That was good news, but evidently, if desperate enough, a person will find a way to obtain one.

But for what purpose?

Could it be Dale Morris arming himself? He'd been chased today and had to know we were searching the ship to find him. Or was it the assassin? Having missed twice now, was he so invested in seeing the job through he would make a third attempt? A handgun at close range would do the trick.

With an unwelcome thud, my heart sent a spasm of fear through my body. Like I was moving in slow motion, I couldn't get my body to move fast enough. I needed to see the Prime Minister. Call it sixth sense, call it intuition, but whatever it is, I knew he was about to get shot.

Worse yet, I was wrong about the PM not recognising Stephanie. They were meeting at that very second, Prime Minister Filipovic leaning forward as he shook her hand. He turned to face the cameras so they could capture the moment. I knew I was shouting, but I couldn't hear the words coming from my mouth over the clamouring of blood rushing through my head.

My warning cries made him and everyone else look my way, but unlike the President of the United States, no pack of secret service agents swarmed to protect him. In fact, yet again his own bodyguard was strangely absent, which is why the bullet hit him.

The Real Target

He was looking right at me when it struck the side of his chest. In reaction to the sound of gunfire, screams filled the air and the banquet room became bedlam. I caught a glimpse of the prime minister falling backwards, but my eyes were already turning away from him.

He was either mortally wounded or he wasn't. There was no sense in me rushing to get to him either way. A second passed with no second shot following the first. To my mind that meant there wouldn't be one. The assassin had struck again, this time with a stolen handgun taken from one of the ship's own security officers. He got his shot off and, knowing he had but one chance to escape, ran for the exit using the stampeding crowd for cover.

That was my guess, at least, and when I glimpsed a tall man in a white uniform barging through passengers to get out of the banquet room, I knew I was right.

A second shot from outside the banquet room erased all doubt. Not that it gave me any comfort and the sound it made turned the tide of humanity. They'd been rushing to get away, but those nearest the exit now reversed course, desperate to stay inside if the shooter had already left. The ensuing confusion caused a logjam and though I screamed for people to clear a path, there was no hope to control the mob of panicked passengers.

Defeated by them, I could only hope the security officers outside would be able to spot a man who wasn't one of their own. But what was the likelihood of that? They were more likely to see his uniform and assume he was running for good reason. I learned about Ensign Kapur mere seconds ago, so news of his missing uniform would not yet be public knowledge and we take on new crew all the time.

The assassin was going to escape again.

I wanted to rage at the sky, but there was no time for that. Reacting when a firm hand grabbed my right forearm, I was about to fight them off when I realised it was Alistair. He dragged me until I got my feet moving and fought his way through the crowd to get to Prime Minister Filipovic.

Commander Philips was with him along with two other senior officers. I heard someone say the paramedics were on their way and knew the ship's doctors would race to get him to the sickbay. We were hours out from Honolulu, but within range of a helicopter if surgery at a fully equipped operating room could save his life.

With so many people pressed in around him, I couldn't see anything beyond the downed politician's feet, but pressing in close I found Stephanie. Jermaine was about as close to her as he could be, protecting her with his body. He looked relieved to see me.

"Are you okay? Did you see the shooter?" I grabbed her arms and spat questions in her face.

"It nearly hit me," she blurted. "I felt it go past my arm." She sounded detached from reality and I needed but a moment to realise she was in shock. The attention of everyone was on the prime minister, but Stephanie had been standing right next to him when the bullet hit. She'd been shaking his hand, I recalled, and a worry that had been plaguing my thoughts for hours shouted a message loud and clear inside my head.

The Molovian prime minister was never the target.

The Truth of It

Stephanie's eyes were focused on nothing, her mind undoubtedly racing so fast she couldn't keep up. I didn't know whether she needed a stiff brandy or a slap to the face, so chose neither.

"Let's sit you down before you fall down." I took her to the first chair I could find.

"Oh, Lord. I think I might be sick," she mumbled, a hand to her face as though to catch it.

I helped to get her head between her knees and looked around for a steward. The panic was subsiding, the danger seemingly past though all around me eyes were wide like dinner plates and couples clung to each other.

I could hear the prime minister's wife wailing and cursing him for being so cavalier with his security. She wanted to know where his bodyguard was and so did I. It was a question for later though, because I needed to talk to Stephanie first.

Locating a steward, I left her for a moment to get a glass of water. They all carry soft drinks for those who do not want the alcohol.

"Here, drink this." I shoved it under her nose and got her to sip some.

Giving her a few seconds to recover - goodness knows she deserved them - gave me a chance to weave my head around and get a look between people's legs. To my great surprise, the prime minister was sitting up. I expected that he would be lying on his back and would have his wound exposed, but he had removed only his jacket.

Bright red stained the left side of his white shirt from about three inches below his nipple and down to his belt, but apart from looking a little pale, he appeared unbothered by his injury.

In some ways it reinforced my belief that he was not the target.

Taking a deep breath through my nose, I brought my attention back to Stephanie. Getting down onto my knees, I made eye contact with her.

"Did Dale ever threaten that he would kill you if you left him?" She'd suggested it earlier when she talked about his views of the only way a marriage could end, but that didn't mean he'd ever said the words.

She choked out a sigh. "All the time. He said it before we got married, but I was so blind back then I thought he was just trying to say something romantic. Wait …" What I was really asking her filtered through.

"You were the one the arrow hit, Stephanie. You were right there when the dumbbell smashed into the deck and the bullet that hit Prime Minister Filipovic only just missed you." I let that sink in for a moment before adding, "These weren't politically motivated assassination attempts, Stephanie. I think this was your husband."

Her hand went to her mouth, and she gasped. Then almost before I could catch her, Stephanie's eyes rolled up into her head and she fainted.

"A little help?" I begged, supporting her weight when she fell forward into me. I was on my knees still and though she can't weigh more than a hundred pounds on a heavy day, I still wasn't picking her up without some help.

Her body rose as if by magic, and I looked up to find Jermaine cradling her like a baby.

"Do you really think she is the target, Madam?"

I genuinely did. It had been bothering me for hours. Possibly even since the first assassination attempt missed from such close range. A professional assassin wouldn't miss. Allowing that the prime minister's rival wasn't behind it and the would-be killer could be an amateur motivated to kill his nation's leader for some unfathomable political reason, it still made more sense that Radovan Filipovic was never the target.

Dale Morris came after his wife when she fled their home. How he found out where she was going was arbitrary. The point is he followed her with one goal in mind: to take her life for daring to leave him.

I viewed it as good news. It meant I could relax about a political brouhaha. Proving Stephanie's husband was behind it all might cost Radovan Filipovic the election. When the truth came out his opponent, Lisik Ramovich, would have a field day.

I looked at the PM now. The same pack of photographers were taking shots of him. The paramedics were with him, the oxygen mask and heart monitor making it all seem more dangerous and credible. The pictures and footage – I could see the guy with the video camera making sure he captured it all – would be news headlines within the hour.

But the wave of support would crash when his country learned the truth.

None of that was my problem. Stephanie was. I called to get the paramedics' attention.

"Got a fainter," I stated simply. "The bullet almost hit her."

Stephanie's eyes fluttered open. She was still in Jermaine's unyielding arms, but he lowered her to the deck to meet the paramedic. They were about to move the prime minister, but could spare the time for one of them to check on the floppy woman.

"Stephanie, I'm sending you to the sickbay. Dale won't be able to find you there. You'll stay there until we flush him out and hand him over to the Honolulu police."

"There's really no need," she tried to protest.

"I think there is." This wasn't a conversation. "We will dock in …" I checked my watch, "less than five hours. You can watch TV and hang out with the nurses. This will be over before you know it."

"No, I don't …"

I shot her a warning look that shut her up. There were enough challenges. Taking her off the playing board just made sense. Secure below decks where the passengers cannot easily go, she would be safe.

How silly I am.

Itchy Skull

Just like the previous attempted murders, the assassin slipped away. In the confusion that erupted the moment he fired his stolen gun, he vanished. Having left the banquet room, it would take but a moment to remove his tunic. Don a pair of sunglasses, slip into a restroom and emerge wearing a hoody over the top … however he did it, he was gone.

I had reported the man I saw running from the room, but I couldn't be certain I was looking at the right person. But things *had* changed. The list of suspects had narrowed to one. All we needed to do now was catch him.

"I guess it makes sense," said Alistair in response to my explanation. "Though it's hard to believe anyone would go to such lengths to hurt a person just for ending a relationship."

"Remember Hennessey?" I brought up the name of his former fiancé. The crazy cow came on board as part of a plot to ruin my life. She failed, obviously, but came very close to destroying my relationship with Alistair.

He shuddered and conceded my point. "Very well. Commander Jandl has his photograph, yes?"

"Indeed. So does everyone else, but they are not yet aware how dangerous I consider Dale Morris to be. I need to meet with Commander Jandl. Stephanie will be safe in the sickbay, so now that we can rule out the need to protect the prime minister, we can focus on finding the one man who has been eluding the search teams for more than a day."

"Very good." Alistair leaned down to kiss my cheek, made sure no one was looking, and gave my bottom a pat.

I swatted at his hand, but he was too fast and moved it out of range.

Barbie appeared next to me. She still had Justin with her. "Do you want me to go to the sickbay with Stephanie? I can keep her company so she's with someone she sort of knows, at least."

She has such a kind heart, but with all our new friend had been through, I wanted to offer her some news that would distract her once her husband was in custody.

"Sweetie, instead of that, can you delve into her employment and academic record, please? The poor woman needs a job that challenges her and pays well enough that she can start thinking about what's next."

Justin asked, "Is there anything I can do to help?"

I touched his arm. "Justin, I'm so sorry I brought you into this mess. I had rather hoped this would be a relaxed affair where we could get to know each other."

"That would have been nice."

In total I had spent only a handful of minutes in his company, and shared a few hundred words, but I could already tell Justin was a sweet old man with genuine good intentions.

I needed to go, but in parting I told him, "There will be other opportunities. Let me get ahead of the current dramas and maybe we will find time to share a meal in Honolulu."

"That's sounds lovely, but my time in Hawaii is already accounted for."

"Oh." I hadn't expected that. Guessing he had family to visit, and hoping that was the case, the paramedics were leaving and I was going with them.

"But once I am back on the ship, I will have all the time in the world," he called as I started to move away.

I gave him a quick thumbs up rather than shout across the room. With Jermaine at my side, I left the banquet room with the paramedics, Stephanie, and the prime minister with his entire entourage. The paramedics wanted the prime minister to go on the gurney so they could wheel him down to the sickbay, but in what looked to me like yet another staged photo opportunity, he refused in favour of Stephanie.

I believe the correct collective term for a group of reporters is a gathering of quills, but whether I am right or wrong about that, the same gaggle of Molovian press snapped away to capture their head of nation wounded and bloody, yet deferring aid to a woman who fainted.

Uncharitably, I felt convinced he was only doing it for the optics, but he walked all the way to the elevators and rode them down. I saw him wince a few times, but not once did he ask for any additional support.

There wasn't enough room in the elevator for all the reporters, but he made sure the man with the video camera accompanied him along with an attractive woman in her thirties who jabbered constantly to report what was being shown.

I stayed quiet, keeping watch over Stephanie. Once she was safe, I would focus everything on Commander Jandl and the entire horde of ship's security. We could wait until we docked to find Dale Morris, but I had no patience for that. The elusive wife beater was going ashore in handcuffs.

Interrupting my thoughts, Stephanie asked, "What deck are we going to?"

"Six," I replied. "It's the same place you were in yesterday." Saying it aloud made me question how many times she must have visited her local accident and emergency centre back home. I'd known her a little more than twenty-four hours and this was the second time she needed medical attention at her husband's hands.

At the paramedic's insistence, she laid her head back down and rested. We were nearly there.

I hung around with Stephanie until Dr Davis was ready to see her. He took no more than a few minutes to confirm Stephanie was perfectly okay, but he understood my desire to leave her in the sickbay. There were other places I could put her that would be equally secure, yet setting them up and arranging for someone to be with her would eat up time. Time that could be better spent in pursuit of the perpetrator.

Across the room, Hideki worked on the prime minister. He needed stitches and something for the pain, but I saw his wound from across the room and it looked quite superficial. It bled plenty, but the bullet gouged the flesh on one side of his ribs, failing to penetrate his chest at all.

Dr Davis argued about letting the reporters in, but didn't care enough to ask security to kick them out. So while Hideki worked and the camera rolled, I made my way to the PM's bedside.

"How are you feeling, Radovan?"

He managed a tired smile and an almost laugh. "Like a man who knows what it feels like to represent the will of a nation. Our enemies, foreign and domestic, financial or otherwise, will come at us. They will attack, they will wound, and they will find us more resilient than they could ever have imagined. I bleed for Molovia and will do so again if the people let me."

It was not the first time I found myself acknowledging his skill as a speaker. In just a few words, he'd delivered a speech that was almost a manifesto. It had no content, yet the power of his determination shone through. His country would vote for him, of that I had very little doubt. The election would be a landslide.

The back of my head itched.

"Where is your bodyguard?"

"Absent again," spat the prime minister's wife. She stood by his side, holding his hand and looking annoyed or possibly even angry. "You should fire him and get someone competent, Radi."

I couldn't agree more, but the prime minister was ready to argue.

"I gave him the time off, darling. He escorted us to the lunch, but once there we were in the company of more than a dozen of the ship's security guards." He swung his face to meet my eyes. "I should have been perfectly safe. Wouldn't you agree, Mrs Fisher?"

The cameraman shifted to make sure I was in the frame and I felt a little heat come to my cheeks.

"We are investigating the circumstances of this attack and will know more once there has been time to collate evidence." I congratulated myself on giving an answer that avoided answering his question. He was right, of course, he ought to have been safe, yet Dale Morris managed to get in to take a shot at his wife.

Again my skull itched. I was missing something. I wanted to tell the Molovian Prime Minister that he was wrong. That there was no assassin, but I couldn't do that on camera if there was a chance I could be wrong.

Excusing myself, I said, "On that note, I really must get back to work." He looked like he had other things he wanted to say, and I was glad to escape. With a final word to Stephanie, telling her to sit tight and that it would all be over soon, I left with Jermaine.

Morris Bail Bonds

I was on my way to liaise with Commander Jandl when my phone rang. Seeing Molly's name on the screen, I thumbed the button to connect the call and pressed it to my ear.

"Molly."

"You know those two bounty hunter types you told us about?"

"Yes."

"They just passed us. They look dodgy as anything. Should we follow them? I'm with Sam," she added.

"No. They're not important."

Or were they? On the face of it, they were just another odd occurrence on board a cruise ship that has always got something weird or criminal going on. But they kept popping up.

"Wait," I said before Molly could respond to my previous instruction. "Where are you?"

"On deck fourteen. We weren't doing anything much so decided to help Commander Jandl search the ship. He needs all the help he can get."

He really did, but there was something about their presence on deck fourteen that bothered me. "Where exactly on deck fourteen?"

The location Molly gave was precisely where I hoped she wouldn't say. The thugs were in the same passageway as Stephanie's new cabin and had previously been spotted close to where her original cabin was located. Were they working for Dale Morris?

I had nothing to connect them. Yet the possibility their unnamed fugitive was his wife struck me as worryingly believable. The last time I spoke with them, Mason let slip that their quarry was a man, but was he brighter than he seemed? Were they really here looking for Stephanie, and said they were after a man to muddy the water? They were right there after we spotted Dale on the escalator. Was that a coincidence? Or were they running interference to help him get away?

I told Molly and Sam to keep their distance, but to follow and not let Mason and Edgar out of their sight. There were too many coincidences for my liking, too many converging paths. I knew I was missing something, but whether the bounty hunters and their fugitive had anything to do with it, I was yet to figure out.

With my phone already in my hand, I placed a call to Barbie.

"Hey, Patty. If you're calling about Stephanie's employment record, I haven't gotten to it yet. Is it urgent?"

"Not as urgent as the next task. Can you look up a pair of bounty hunters for me?" I gave their names. "I'm looking for any connection between them and Stephanie's husband."

"You think he hired them to capture her?"

"Maybe. Let me know what you find."

Call complete, I pushed on to find Commander Jandl.

With my radio he was easy enough to find. Commanding the search team from the crew room on deck nineteen, he now had more than three hundred of the ship's crew involved in the hunt for Dale Morris. To augment the security teams, many of which were already preparing for the landing in Hawaii, chefs, cleaners, stewards, and more found themselves drafted in. No one complained. They all understood this was part of the job. The Aurelia is our home, and our solemn duty as its inhabitants is to protect the guests we invite on board.

Despite the size of the search team, and Commander Jandl's detailed plan to dissect the ship and clear it deck by deck from the bottom up, they were still to find the man in question.

It made me question if Dale Morris was something more than we believed. Listed as a librarian, did he have a military past that gifted him with additional skills? It might explain his ability to evade the search teams and his confidence with weapons. Stephanie said they had been married for three years. That left plenty of time for him to have had a career doing something else before they met.

I thought about calling Barbie again. She would be able to find out one way or another, but my young blonde friend was already looking up the bounty hunters. However, I figured that wouldn't take her long and to accentuate my point, my phone rang. She was talking before I could get it to my ear.

"You were right, Patty."

I wanted to say something flippant about her sentence being redundant because, of course, I was, but I let her continue.

"Mason Searle and Edgar Bruner both work for Morris Bail Bonds. I'm doing a deeper dive now, but if they work for Dale Morris, it's not exactly a giant leap to guess who they are looking for. Will you have them arrested now?"

I probably could, but was that the right move? "Babes, while you are in the researching mood, can you check Dale's past? I want to know if he is ex-forces or something like that. In the file Martin pulled together, he has Dale listed as a librarian. That's clearly not the case. If he falsified the details of his employment to hide that he runs a bounty hunting agency, what other secrets does he have?"

I didn't think his past was all that important, not from the perspective of catching him. I wouldn't be the one pressing charges and trying to make them stick, but knowledge is knowledge and if he was some kind of super soldier, I wanted the crew to know who they were up against.

Barbie said she would get right on it, and I called Molly.

"Patricia?" she whispered into the phone.

"Are you still on them?"

"Yeah. Sam and I are taking it in turns. I'm pretty sure they have no idea we are following. You want us to do something else?"

I told her the news about who they work for. "Sooner or later, they are going to lead us to their boss. They won't find Stephanie because I've squirrelled her away below decks." I chose not to say where she was. The fewer people who know a secret, the easier it is to keep. "But listen, I want you to call Schneider or Deepa ... one of our own. Tell them where you are and get them to replace you. The longer you tail Mason and Edgar, the more likely it is you will be spotted. Get them to come in plain clothes, okay?"

"Roger. I'm on it."

When I put my phone away, Jermaine asked, "Will you pause for lunch, Madam? I haven't seen you eat anything since breakfast."

Eating sounded good, but I just didn't feel there was time.

"Maybe we can swing past the buffet on deck eighteen?" I suggested. "We can grab some fruit." I could tell Jermaine thought I needed something more substantial, but it quickly became moot when my radio came to life.

"All callsigns, this is Dr Davis in sickbay. We have been attacked. Request assistance. Over."

Barbie's Research

Sitting crossed-legged at the desk in Patty's suite, Barbie munched on pistachios, her jaw moving while her eyes remained locked on the screen to her front.

Lady Mary returned from the kitchen where she had fixed herself a gin and tonic and fetched sparkling mineral water for her very boring blonde friend.

"It doesn't taste of anything," she advised, setting the glass down next to Barbie's right hand.

"That's kind of the point, Mary. Gin is tasty and all, but it's chock full of calories. Even if you use slimline tonic."

Lady Mary patted her trim waist. "I think I'm doing okay for an old bird."

Barbie didn't waste her breath arguing. Lady Mary kept a slim core by opting to avoid food half the time. She drank most of her calories and never did any exercise, but now was not the time to point out her dietary deficiencies.

Finding Mason Searle and Edgar Bruner took so few seconds it was barely a challenge at all, but delving into Dale Morris's past, especially if he was trying to keep it hidden, was something into which she could sink her teeth.

"What are you doing?" Lady Mary asked, more to make conversation than because she had any interest.

"Well," Barbie snapped open another pistachio and popped it into her mouth. "I'm looking at Dale's employment record, but there is nothing here to suggest he is anything other than a librarian. There is no mention of his bail bond business, which is odd. But not nearly so strange as this." She zoomed in on a portion of the screen and pointed to it with a delicate index finger.

Lady Mary squinted. "Yes, that is very interesting. What am I looking at?"

Barbie rolled her eyes. Lady Mary needed reading glasses, but they sat in the drawer in her room because she didn't like people to see her wearing them.

"I'm on the ship's central registry. It shows all kinds of information. I was looking at Stephanie's husband to see if he booked with a credit card. He did, of course, and I was going to use that information plus a few other details I've been able to glean to call his credit card firm and find out a little more."

"You can do that?"

"It's not entirely legal, but I can claim to be his wife, and with his date of birth, social security number, knowledge of recent transactions and such, there's no reason why they wouldn't talk to me."

"Okay, so what do you hope to learn from them?"

"Nothing."

Lady Mary frowned deeply and chewed her bottom lip. "I'm not sure I follow."

"Sorry. I mean I was planning to find out enough that I could then call the VA."

"VA?"

"Veterans' Association. If he was military, they will be able to confirm it, but they won't talk to me unless I know enough to convince them I'm his wife. I can tell them he has recently died and ask about pension benefits. That might sound a little callous …"

"Not at all, dear. The man hits his wife and appears to be on the ship with the sole aim of ending her life. Do whatever you want to him."

Barbie held up her index finger and pointed at the screen again. "Anyway, I was trying to do all that when I found this. It's the date he booked his cruise."

Lady Mary moved her head closer to the screen, then backed away until it was just about in focus.

"I see it. You obviously think it's significant."

"I do. He booked it two days before Stephanie."

Sickbay

The call from Dr Davis got me running, and the radio chatter bouncing back and forth the instant he cleared the airwaves told me plenty of others were heading there too.

I had to kick off my heels – they were impossible to run in, and shouted, "Leave them!" when Jermaine reversed course to collect them. Proving his speed, he got the shoes and caught up with me in a matter of seconds.

It was Dale. It had to be. I stupidly thought Stephanie would be safe below the passenger decks, but her husband managed to find her anyway. Just who was this guy? I'd left two security officers with the prime minister, so he'd not only overpowered them, but the sickbay staff as well. There was almost always a doctor and at least two nurses stationed there regardless of the time of day.

A chill thought crept over me. What if I was wrong? What if it wasn't Dale and there really was an assassin after Radovan Filipovic?

Jumping on the radio, I blurted, "Dr Davis, this is Patricia. Is anyone hurt?"

"No, but Stephanie Morris is missing! Someone hit me from behind, locked the nurses in the dispensary, and when I came to she was gone."

I was dialling her number before Dr Davis finished speaking. Running at speed had my breath pulling already, but Stephanie could put up with my heavy breathing just so I could know she was okay. Except she didn't answer the phone. The lack of response drove a wedge of fear through me.

If I was right about her husband, he was on board to kill her and probably planned to step off the ship in Hawaii without a care in the world. There were names I wanted to call him, and only just managed to keep them to myself when I stuffed the phone back into my bag.

Jermaine and I arrived at the nearest elevator bank out of breath and just as the doors were opening. Half a dozen lieutenants from the ship's security team were rushing to get inside. They saw me coming and held the doors. Messages were pinging back and forth across their radios and mine, mostly from Commander Jandl who seized control of the situation to deploy a portion of his crew to deck six. When I stepped into the elevator he was quizzing Dr Davis about the prime minister, but the doors shut and I didn't get to hear his reply – the stupid radios don't work inside the steel box.

Anxious to know more, I was poised to ask for an update when the elevator doors opened, and I heard what sounded like Lieutenant Horobin reporting. "He's back in his cabin, sir. I escorted him there myself and we are stationed outside his door."

We burst from the elevator at a sprint, all racing around to get to the crew-only elevator that would take us down to deck six.

I squeezed the radio's send button.

"This is Patricia." It's actually kind of cool to go by one name. I feel like I could be on a par with Beyonce, Adele, or Sting. "Are you talking about Prime Minister Filipovic? Over."

"Yes. This is Horobin, Mrs Fisher. He's in his suite. Whatever happened in the sickbay, he missed it. Over."

Okay, so that was a relief, yet it also confirmed my fear that Dale came for Stephanie. I was mad and sad at the same time. So much effort into keeping her out of his grasp and he found her anyway. The crew were searching the ship, clearing it one deck at a time, and all the while he was on the crew decks where no one thought to look. When I looked at the problem from the other side, it was so utterly obvious why no one had been able to find him.

I fell into the next elevator, which once again the younger men were holding open for me, and lost the radio signal for a second time. Mercifully, we only had one deck to descend, and spilled onto deck six about twelve seconds later.

A little more running, all of which made me wish I was in my Sketchers still, and we burst into the sickbay to find we were not the first to arrive. A dozen crew got there ahead of us. Not just members of the security team, but engineers, someone from the bursar's office, and I recognised two of the water sports team. In charge was my very own Lieutenant Commander Baker.

Martin saw me arrive and signalled for everyone else to stop talking. "Thank you, everyone. I appreciate your swift response. We have it from here."

I pushed through as most of them turned to leave.

Dr Davis was in a chair with Nurse Helmcamp tending to a wound on his head. There was blood on his collar and down his shirt. From the blow to his head, no doubt. He looked more angry than hurt, so I dismissed my concern and focused on the sickbay itself.

It looked more or less exactly as I left it, which made no sense. If Dale came for Stephanie, knocked out Dr Davis and took her by force, why were none of the tables overturned? How come there was no mess? At all?

I went straight to Dr Davis. "What happened?"

Nurse Helmcamp, a tall Austrian woman with blond hair turning grey and an unforgiving expression, had the good doctor leaning forward and his head facing the deck. She tutted when he tilted it back to look at me.

"No clue. Sorry. I was writing up notes on the prime minister when someone hit me from behind. Whoever it was, I never even heard them enter."

I shared a look with Jermaine. He knew my theory about Dale and what sort of training he might have. Not expecting to achieve anything by doing so, I called Stephanie's phone again. It rang and rang before switching to voicemail.

Feeling defeated, I gripped the nearest bed and used it to keep myself upright. I hadn't eaten enough, there had been far too little sleep in the last couple of days, and it felt like I'd spent half the day running. Fatigue ruled, and my mind was a foggy mess.

Stephanie's husband had her and he could be anywhere on the entire ship. The deck-by-deck search failed to roust him from his hiding spot because he is better at this game than I am. I wallowed in self-pity for five seconds, but not a moment longer. My top lip curled, angry at myself as much as I was aiming it at Dale.

Pushing away from the bed, I reached for my radio.

"Patricia Fisher for Commander Jandl, over."

I updated him with my suspicions. He was going to have to start his search again and employ a separate team to explore the crew decks. That itself was a near impossible task with all the engineering gubbins and vast storerooms, but it had to be attempted. They were looking for a man and a woman now. At least I hoped they were. Dale's best bet was to kill Stephanie quickly. If she was conscious, I felt certain she would scream for help and fight to get free, but he took her from the sickbay rather than kill her the first chance he got and that gave me cause to hope.

There was nothing more I could do below decks, and I felt it was my duty to let the Molovian PM know there was no assassin out to end his life. His wife would be relieved at least. Besides, my insides were knotted with worry and I needed something to do.

Good Shot

"I might be the only person in history to congratulate the man who shot him for being such a good aim."

Grigore Volantin acknowledged the compliment with a dip of his head and said, "I'm sure I'm not the only person in history to happily shoot a politician."

Radovan Filipovic laughed, but winced the moment he did. "Goodness, that hurts. No more jokes, please." His re-election was assured and he felt truly jubilant. It could be argued that faking a third attempt on his life was unnecessary, but the photographs of his bloody shirt and the rehearsed words he made to look spontaneous were the final icing on the cake. Lisik Ramovich was history. With one hand pressing lightly on the site of his wound, he met his bodyguard with a serious expression. "You got away cleanly?"

"I believe so."

"You believe so? Have you any idea what would happen to my re-election hopes if you were discovered?"

They talked in hushed tones, not wanting to be overheard. That made it hard for the prime minister to put sufficient emphasis in his words, but the point came across all the same. His wife was resting in their bedroom, and the butler was in his adjoining cabin, out of the way but available at a moment's notice.

"Yes, I think I can figure out what would happen, but we have discussed this already. There is no way to ever be one hundred percent sure. For the third assassination attempt I wore a wig, a false nose, and makeup to alter the shape of my face. The uniform allowed me to blend in with the other security officers when the crowd panicked. When I fired the arrow, I was off the helipad and inside the ship long before the security officers could even figure out where the shot came from, and I wore a disguise when I dropped the dumbbell. If they suspected anything, that Patricia Fisher woman would be knocking at your door."

"Then pray tell me why she just asked me where you were again?"

Grigore shrugged. "So maybe she suspects something. So long as she cannot prove anything ..."

"You were supposed to take her off the playing board."

"And make it look like an accident. That's not an easy thing to achieve, so yes, my first attempt failed."

"You tried to drop a lifeboat on her head, man!"

"I'm fairly sure that would have taken her off the playing board."

Prime Minister Filipovic bared his teeth. "But I told you what would happen if you killed her. That annoyingly persistent woman is too famous. Her death would be a bigger story than my failed assassination. Nothing can distract the press from my story."

"You want me to try again, or not?" Grigore did nothing to hide the frustration he felt. His boss paid well but was far too demanding and expected perfection. He'd managed to not kill him or anyone else three times in twenty-four hours.

The skills he possessed deserved far greater respect, but his boss was about to be re-elected and he was in line to become the national head of security, a position that came with a fat paycheck and a large house. He could put up with the prime minister for that. Unfortunately, the Airtag he put in her handbag had stopped moving. It was possible she'd simply changed handbags – that was the sort of thing a woman would do in Grigore's experience. It was that or she'd found it and that would make her wary. He wasn't one to underestimate people. That could get you caught or killed.

"No. I think a second attempt would be too risky. Like you say, if she truly suspected anything she would be knocking at my door."

Both men's head snapped sharply around to glare accusingly at the door when someone outside rapped their knuckles against it.

"Hello?" called a voice that was distinctly Patricia Fisher's.

Staged?

The door opened to reveal Prime Minister Filipovic's bodyguard, not Castle the butler as it ought to be. It was the second time he'd opened the door, and I recalled how he'd bumped into me the last time. Theories were forming in my brain and he was right in the middle of them. I couldn't be sure he'd dropped the Airtag in my handbag, and I had not one theory why he would want to drop a lifeboat on me. Like I said earlier, I am missing something.

Dismissing those concerns for now, I said, "Hello. May I come in, please? I have news for the prime minister."

Radovan's voice echoed from within his suite. "Who is it, Grigore? Is that Mrs Fisher I can hear?"

Grigore stepped out of the way to grant me access, and he did so with a small flourish, but I caught his eyes and saw the worry they contained.

Radovan occupied the suite as only a politician can, his ego filling far more space than his short body would suggest possible. Standing to the side of a high-backed armchair, he rested against it with one arm, his stance casual. He had changed from his suit into a polo shirt and light woollen sweater yet still looked very much the statesman.

"Patricia, please do come in." He paid no attention to Jermaine, acting as though he wasn't even there. "Are you coming to check on me? Or do you have information regarding the assassin you wish to share?" He moved in front of the armchair and indicated the one set opposite. "Please, sit. I wish to hear all you have to say. I have arranged a press conference to take place on the quayside when we arrive in Honolulu. It seems I have become almost a folk legend back home. The man who survived three assassination attempts."

I lowered myself onto the seat but chose not to relax into it. I wasn't planning to stay long.

"You appear in fine form for a man who was shot less than an hour ago."

He cracked a smile and an almost laugh which brought a wince to his lips.

"Ooh." He pressed a hand to the wound. "Yes, well, I think I was extremely lucky. The bullet grazed my ribs. Tell me, though, how is Miss Morris? She appeared to have recovered, but I wasn't able to speak with her again before I left the sickbay."

He always asked the right questions. Ones that made him come across as selfless. Ignoring that I believed it to be a façade he wore, his question cued up my revelation quite neatly.

"Thank you for asking. I'm afraid Miss Morris is in rather dire straits." Radovan blinked in confusion, so before he could ask what I meant, I ploughed onwards. "I'm afraid we have misconstrued the assassination attempts, Prime Minister."

"How so?"

Grigore moved around the room to stand behind his boss. He also wanted to hear my reasoning.

PRIME SHOT

"The person who shot Stephanie Morris with an arrow was not, in fact, aiming at you." Confusion swam across the prime minister's features. "Stephanie Morris is on the run from her husband. He is an abusive man with a history of marital violence. He followed her to the Aurelia and has been trying to kill her ever since. I believe he dropped the dumbbell, and it was he who shot you today while aiming at her. I'm fairly certain he was behind the lifeboat that almost crushed me earlier today." Actually, I wasn't all that sure about the last part and was becoming less sure by the moment.

The prime minister's face was contorted into a deep frown that grew angrier before my eyes.

"What is the meaning of this?" he demanded, flecks of spittle leaving his mouth as the words rushed from them.

I felt Jermaine stiffen.

"How dare you suggest these attacks were anything other than attempts to change the course of my re-election. This was nothing to do with anyone's husband! This is the work of my opponent, Lisik Ramovich."

"I'm sorry, Radovan, but ..."

"Radovan? You think you have the right to address me by my first name when you come into my suite and accuse me of ... what? Staging the whole thing? The papers list you as a legendary sleuth, but you are nothing but a hack."

I narrowed my eyes and gave it a couple of seconds to be sure he was finished.

"Prime Minister Filipovic, it's refreshing to see the politician fade away and the real person emerge."

"How dare you!"

"With great ease, I can assure you."

"I think it is time for you to leave." He raised his right hand in a gesture that was supposed to get his bodyguard moving. "Show them the door, Grigore."

Barely contained violence, ready to be dispensed at a moment's notice, radiated off Jermaine. Grigore was undoubtedly a capable bodyguard, but he did not move the instant his boss gave the command.

Clasping my handbag, I rose to my feet. "Thank you. We can see ourselves out."

Waves of masculine energy filled the gap between the two bodyguards, but Jermaine turned away and came with me when I started toward the exit. With a quicker pace, he reached it before me, holding it so I could leave ahead of him, but I was only vaguely aware of my passage from the prime minister's suite. My mind was elsewhere.

It would be easy to put the prime minister's outburst down to his concerns over his re-election hopes. I could see how damaging it would be if the press at home reported the assassination attempts were nothing of the sort. His opponent, currently vilified, would at once be exonerated and find himself armed with ammunition. But that wasn't what I was thinking.

I was thinking about the word 'staged'.

He questioned if I thought he had staged the assassination attempts. Why would he do that? I wanted to give the question more thought, but I still had to save Stephanie. She was on the ship somewhere, held captive by her husband, and under threat of death. Would she be able to calm him now they were together?

Adrift on a cloud of questions, I hadn't picked a direction to walk when I left the prime minister, but found myself aimed in the general direction of my own suite.

"Madam?" Jermaine's voice invaded my thoughts. "Can I implore you to eat something? It has been a great many hours since your last meal."

I knew he was right. I'd promised to stop by the buffet on deck eighteen, but we found ourselves diverted by the attack on the sickbay. Pausing to eat still felt frivolous. Dale could be doing anything to Stephanie, but it was only a short walk to my place where we could grab something portable from the kitchen.

Accepting that it would take but a moment, and that I really ought to eat, I was turning my head to agree with Jermaine when I heard something unyieldingly solid strike against something made of flesh. I looked into Jermaine's eyes in time to see them roll upward into his head.

His body sagged, the muscles keeping it upright no longer willing to play ball. Like a tree being felled, he pitched forward and to the left. I grabbed him, doing my best to control his fall though I discovered he is even heavier than he looks. At six feet four inches, he is tall and has thick muscle developed by time in the gym. If pushed to guess I would estimate his weight to be two hundred and thirty pounds, but it could be more than that.

It took all my strength to control his fall to the deck, but the moment he was down I turned my attention to the man who hit him. Obscured by Jermaine's broad shoulders until he collapsed, was Mason Searle, the butt ugly monkey turd of a bounty hunter. In his hands he clasped a fire extinguisher, a device with enough heft to knock my butler unconscious.

He'd been tucked in an alcove formed by two bulkheads that probably ran around electrics or pipe works or something. There was no way to see him until he stepped out and by then it was too late.

Grinning at me, he let go with one hand to let it fall to his side. "Scream and I'll kill your butler long before anyone can come to rescue you."

Really Badly Wrong

Lady Mary asked, "What is that thing you are looking at, dear?" To demonstrate how captivating Barbie's research proved to be, she'd emptied her gin glass more than fifteen minutes ago and hadn't even thought about refilling it.

Barbie had her left leg curled beneath her body, her lips slightly open and a concerned look creasing her brow.

"This isn't right," she murmured. "I need to tell Patty."

"Tell her what, sweetie? I'm not following."

Without taking her eyes from the screen, Barbie's left arm snaked out to find her phone. It was on the desk to the left of her laptop. Only once it was in her hand and the home screen swam into life did she glance to make sure she was calling the right person.

Tapping the green button to make the call, and the speaker icon so she could talk hands free, she waited for Patricia to answer.

When it continued to ring, she said, "Come on, Patty. This is important."

"What's important, dear? What am I missing? This looks like a military training record."

"That's because it is," Barbie replied. Frustrated, she killed the call and tried again. "Patty asked me to find out if Stephanie's husband had any military training. She thinks he's been able to evade the deck-by-deck search, that he shot an arrow yesterday and a gun today. She also believes he broke into the sickbay and overwhelmed the doctor and nurses all without being seen."

"That's right," agreed Lady Mary, wondering why Barbie was reiterating what they already knew.

"Well, Patty has it wrong. Really badly wrong. I don't think I've ever said this before, but she has been duped and if I don't let her know that she has the whole thing about face, she is going to find herself in a heck of a lot of trouble." The phone switched over to voicemail. "Dang it!"

Barbie bounced out of her chair with enough force to send it flying back across the room. It stopped when it hit the couch, waking the pair of snoozy dachshunds. Not that they were bothered enough to get up.

Lady Mary squinted at the screen and used the roller thingy on the mouse to scroll back up. She'd never really seen the use for computers and had never thought it necessary to own one. People with jobs owned them. However, her husband spent most of his life with his face glued to the screen of his as he wrote his little stories, and she knew the basics of how to make one work.

Scrolling back to the top of the document, she looked at the name appended to it: Mason.

Barbie slid on her running shoes and slipped her phone into the stretchy pocket on her left hip.

"If Patty isn't answering the phone, I'm going to have to go find her."

Lady Mary's eyes were glued to the screen, but she managed to say, "How are you going to do that, dear?"

"I'll find the first person with a radio and tell everyone the truth."

Lady Mary was about to ask, 'What truth?' when she saw it. Her mouth opened and closed a couple of times before Barbie opened the door to leave.

"Wait!" she called. Placing her empty gin glass on the desk and running to catch the lithe blonde woman. "Wait for me! I don't want to miss this!"

Ambush

My phone rang in my handbag, but I didn't dare try to get to it. Mason had just told me he would kill Jermaine if I called for help. As threats go it was quite effective.

The Aurelia was close enough to Hawaii now that passengers would be lining the outer decks to see the magnificent view. Or they would be in the cabins packing to be ready to go ashore. I could predict their behaviour because I'd seen it so many times. It meant the inner passageways were relatively empty and that Mason had picked a good place for his ambush.

However, a passenger or crew member could happen along at any moment. That was predictable too, so I just needed to stall him for a while and hope for the best. The sound of a shoe scuffing on the deck revealed Edgar who came around the corner to join us.

"Any trouble?"

"No trouble at all," Mason continued to grin at me. "He's big, but he's not indestructible. Now we just have to deal with her."

My phone rang off for a second time, and when it fell silent I could hear my radio making muffled noises inside my handbag. It was on the deck a couple of feet away where I'd dropped it to grab Jermaine. My glance gave me away and Edgar got to it first.

"I think I'll have that, thank you." He picked it up and slipped it over his shoulder. It did not go with his outfit.

"We need to get this one out of sight," said Mason.

"What about him?" asked Edgar, clearly meaning Jermaine.

Mason gave it a second of thought. "Throw him overboard?"

"Nah. We'll get spotted. There's a restroom around the corner. Let's stuff him in there."

I was still on my knees, protecting Jermaine with my body, though I knew there was little I could do against the two rough men. To drive that point home, Edgar grabbed me around the back of my neck with one meaty hand and used it to haul me to my feet.

"Here, hold on," Mason complained. "How come you get to manhandle the old lady and I have to shift this deadweight?"

Old lady? I was going to kick Mason in the pants the first chance I got. Ignoring his insult, I suggested, "It will be easier if you both do it. I won't run away. Honest."

Mason eyed his partner. "It would be easier with two."

"And if only one of you is going to move him, it should be Edgar. He's clearly stronger." I reached up to squeeze his bicep.

Mason bristled. "No, he isn't!"

Edgar rolled his eyes. "She's messing with us, dummy. The moment I let her go she'll be off down this passageway like Merlene Ottey."

"She said she wouldn't." Mason didn't want to shift Jermaine by himself.

Edgar gave my neck a squeeze and pushed me ahead of him. "Luck of the draw. I've got the old lady. You get the bodyguard. Come on, we haven't got all day."

Tutting, griping, and using language a lady shouldn't have to hear, Mason managed to roll Jermaine onto his back and sit him up. Crouching behind him, he hooked his arms under Jermaine's so he could drag him backwards.

With the added time I created by stalling them, it was now more than a minute since they attacked. More than enough time to get into position, I felt.

"Freeze scumbag!" yelled Molly, leaping from a side passage. She was still in uniform and had her sidearm drawn. She pointed it first at Edgar and then at Mason.

Mason dropped Jermaine who flopped unceremoniously back to the deck in a heap.

"You're cute," said Mason, rubbing the stubble on his chin. "But I don't have time for a stripper right now. You could come by my cabin later though ..."

Molly's face wrinkled. "Ewwww." But she wasn't swayed or distracted by his lewd remarks. "Put your hands up dirtbags. Or don't. I have always wanted to know what it would be like to shoot an actual person instead of a cardboard target and I'm sure Mrs Fisher will forgive me."

"I shall applaud you, my dear."

"Hear that?" Molly switched her aim from Mason to Edgar. "I will get a round of applause for shooting you. Now, unhand Mrs Fisher and get on your knees."

Mimicking Molly's move, Sam jumped out from the other side of the cross passage.

"Do as she says, ball bags!" Scumbag and dirtbag might be acceptable terms when dealing with criminal types, but I wasn't entirely sold on Sam's choice. He was also in uniform, but unlike Molly, he wasn't armed and the effect wasn't quite the same. His wrestler's pose, arms out and fingers splayed was the toughest in his arsenal, but against Mason and Edgar, it had the wrong effect.

Mason fixed his gaze on me. "What is this? The circus? First some Buffy the Vampire Slayer wannabe threatens to shoot me and now you have a mongo on your team? How are we supposed to take you seriously?"

Calling me an old lady is one thing, but no one gets to say bad things about Sam. I was quite looking forward to what was going to happen next.

"Hey, I'm still holding this gun," said Molly.

Mason swung his head back in her direction. "Yeah, little girl, but you're not going to use it. Not without wetting your knickers."

Molly sniggered. "Well, you're right about one thing." She put her gun back into its holster. "I'm not going to use it. There's too much chance I might hit the people behind you."

Mason pulled a bored face. "Really? The old look behind you trick? As if I'm going to fall for that."

Edgar wasn't paying any attention to me. He probably figured his hand around my neck was enough to make me behave, which is why he didn't see when I lifted my right arm up high, clamped my left hand over my right fist and drove it into his gut with all my might.

He didn't double over or cry out in pain, but the blow jolted him enough that his grip weakened. I dropped to the deck, creating a clear line of fire if anyone felt a need to shoot, because I'd been watching Sam's eyes.

People dismiss him as though Downs means he is incapable, but constantly being underestimated gives him an edge. While Mason and Edgar watched Molly, Sam let me know there was someone coming from behind us. Together with Molly, their job was to distract. She could have shot one or both of them, but discharging one's firearm must always be the last resort. If they can resolve a situation without shooting anyone, they must do so.

I think it was Molly's grin that finally convinced Mason to look, but by then it was too late, and Schneider was already swinging a haymaker. The tall Austrian hit the bounty hunter full in his face, splatting his nose and lips. The punch drove his head backwards, lifting him from the deck so he crashed back into the wall and slithered down it, clearly unconscious.

I rushed to Jermaine's side just as Deepa swept Edgar's legs. He went over backward to land on his shoulders and neck with Molly, Sam, and Deepa all diving on top. In seconds he was face down with his hands cuffed behind his back and Deepa was talking to the ship's paramedics.

On the back of Jermaine's head, a goose egg sized lump leaked a little blood where the fire extinguisher broke the skin. He was breathing steadily, and I could say that I wasn't overly worried about him, but what I really mean is that I believed he would be okay. Concussed perhaps, out of action for a while, certainly, but I doubted the knock to his head would prove fatal.

Since there was nothing I could do for him, I turned my rage on Edgar.

Kneeling on his back, I twisted his head to one side so he could see it was me and growled into his ear. "I want to know where Dale Morris is and so help me if you don't tell me I'm going to ..."

"I've got no idea!" he squeaked in a tone that was convincing enough to silence me. "We've been looking for him ever since we got on the ship. Wherever he's hiding, it's beaten us."

"What are you talking about? You work for him!" I adjusted my position and started to root through his pockets. His phone would be here somewhere and Dale's number would be in it.

"Work for ... You think I work for Dale Morris?"

I said, "Yes," but even to my ears I sounded unconvinced.

"Patty!"

The sound of Barbie's voice filled the passageway. I twisted my body to see her running toward me.

"Can you go a little slower, please?" protested Lady Mary, ambling along twenty yards behind her. "Not all of us have springs in our legs!" She aimed her cry at Barbie's back, but my young blonde friend wasn't stopping for anything.

"Patty, you've got it all back to front!" she shouted. "Dale Morris isn't the owner of Morris Bail Bonds."

A cog clicked into place and I saw it all.

Slightly Deranged

Like a veil lifting, I suddenly saw why things hadn't been making sense. That constant sense that I was missing something came down to one simple fact. Stephanie Morris wasn't on the run from her husband. He was running from her.

The man I heard in her cabin earlier was probably Mason or Edgar. She was out of her cabin last night not because she couldn't sleep, but to search for Dale. Mason and Edgar had been doing the same.

Barbie spotted Jermaine, screeched his name, and fell to her knees at his side. The sound of running boots on the deck told me the paramedics were coming, but my brain was moving too fast now to pay attention to the things happening around me.

Lady Mary wheezed to a halt at my side. "Did she tell you yet? I didn't hear her, so I'll deliver the news. Stephanie Morris is a former member of the SAS. I didn't even know they had those in Australia. She was dishonourably discharged three years ago. There's nothing we could find to indicate why, but she opened Morris Bail Bonds shortly afterward and has been bounty hunting ever since."

Dale Morris hadn't shot his wife with an arrow and he hadn't tried to drop a dumbbell on her head. Dr Davis never heard his attacker enter the sickbay because she was already there. No wonder Stephanie was so coy about her education and employment history. Telling me anything would have given the game away, but she never intended to take a job on the ship. I should have suspected something when he bolted on the escalator and she gave chase. He was trying to get away from a mad woman looking to inflict yet more pain.

Barbie detached herself from Jermaine so the paramedics could get to work. She joined me and Lady Mary.

"You said there were reports of domestic violence at their house, but Darius didn't say which one of them filed the complaint, did he?"

"No," I sighed, "he didn't."

Stephanie manipulated me brilliantly. I fell for every one of her lies. Hooking me with a tale of running away to sea, so reminiscent of my own, was all it took to blind me.

While the paramedics worked on Jermaine and Mason, and more security officers arrived to secure the scene and take Edgar to the brig, Barbie told me about Stephanie's military record and medals. Injured twice in combat, she was a decorated hero, but the photographs she showed me were not ones inflicted by Dale, but the result of enemy action.

Whatever else she was or might have been to her country, she was also completely nuts.

She didn't answer my calls when I phoned her number following the attack at the sickbay, but now I had Edgar's phone and I doubted she would know we'd taken out her employees. I could use it to call her, but to do so would reveal all we knew, and I had a better plan.

I took out my own phone.

"Are you going to tell that woman the game is up?" asked Lady Mary.

"We can arrest her now, right, Mrs Fisher?" said Molly, looking ready to bust some heads.

"And hand her over to the Honolulu PD," added Barbie.

"Actually, I don't think I can. And I'll tell you why." I had everyone's attention, including Edgar's, who twisted his head around to look my way. "What crime has she committed?" I let them consider the question.

As though it were patently obvious, Molly said, "Well she came on board to kill her husband."

"How do we know that?"

Barbie understood what I was saying. "We have no proof. Only hearsay. She hasn't killed him; therefore it could be no more than words."

"But she brought two goons with her. They just attacked you and knocked out Jermaine," argued Lady Mary.

"Which gives us cause to bring charges against the two goons. But Stephanie Morris is yet to do anything that would even land her in cuffs, let alone in jail. We know Dale reported his domestic abuse in the past, but Stephanie is still free to do the same and worse if she catches up to him. To stop her, we must give the police something they can act upon."

Barbie eyed me suspiciously. "Barbie asked, "What are you going to do, Patty?"

"I'm going to let Stephanie try to kill her husband."

Finding Dale

I kissed Jermaine's head before the paramedic's rolled him away. They suspected a mild concussion, but that was for the doctors to diagnose. He was hurt and would be angry that Mason got the better of him, but no one could have detected the bounty hunter tucked out of sight the way he was. I would find him in the sickbay shortly. Right now, though, I had a theory to prove.

"Where are we going, Patty?" asked Barbie, irritated that I wouldn't explain.

"To find Dale Morris," I replied for the third time.

"How?" her eyebrows danced as she tried to figure it out. "They've been searching the ship for him for two days. No one knows where he is."

I pumped my eyebrows and smiled. "No one except me."

She growled her annoyance, which only served to make my cryptic replies more fun.

Lady Mary asked, "Are there any bars on the way to wherever it is we are going? I'm parched."

I had the two of them trailing me along with Molly, Sam, Deepa, and Schneider. I probably didn't need them all, but Stephanie was out there somewhere, and the Aurelia was coming alongside the quay in Honolulu. In less than an hour, passengers would be filing off the ship and that meant she needed to strike soon or risk missing her chance. She had no idea we were onto her, and I was going to use that and her increasing desperation against her.

Barbie fell silent for a beat, but spoke again when she had a new question.

"If Dale wasn't the shooter and it couldn't have been Stephanie who hit herself with an arrow, that means there really is an assassin on board. Shouldn't we be doing something to make sure that prime minister guy gets off the ship alive?"

"Nah. He'll be okay." I made my reply sound utterly unconcerned and disinterested.

"He'll be, okay?" Deepa questioned. "Should I call Commander Jandl? He can ensure a security escort from the ship."

"No need. I believe the PM plans to hold a press conference on the quayside. The ship will make a perfect backdrop to really drive home the dramas he's suffered on board."

"But that will expose him," Schneider pointed out. "It's the perfect time for the assassin to strike again."

"But they won't," I stated with absolute confidence. Just like with Stephanie, it had taken me a while to figure out what I'd seen and what I had failed to see. Until the truth about Stephanie dawned on my addled brain, I couldn't see the truth about the prime minister either. She proved to be the key to both cases, and now it all made perfect sense. Right back when the arrow missed him, I observed that a professional assassin wouldn't have missed.

Unless they intended to.

However, Prime Minister Filipovic was entirely secondary in my list of priorities and weirdly, I had a third case that I was going to solve first.

I led my team to deck fifteen and to a cleaning storeroom where the door opened without a key.

"What are we doing here?" asked Barbie, her nose wrinkling. The room smelled of cleaning products. Not in an unpleasant way, exactly, but it was a little strong.

To get the cleaning carts in and out with ease, the room was fitted with double doors. Most of the carts were out already, the cleaning crews getting ready for the big cabin swap over that occurs every time we make port.

Standing in the doorway, I listened. When I heard nothing, I ventured inside, just to be sure.

"Patty?" Barbie begged. She hates when I won't tell her what I know.

I decided it was time to relent. "The rest of you won't know this, but among the many things that come across my desk, as it were, was the theft of some lunches."

More than one person echoed the word, 'Lunches' with a question mark attached.

"Yup. I'm the ship's detective, so when the cleaning crew put their lunches in their lockers and return to find someone else has eaten them, I'm the one who gets informed."

The point I was trying to make was obvious, but it was Barbie who said it first.

"You think Dale Morris has been stealing the cleaners' lunches."

"It first occurred after we left Sydney. That's where Dale and his psycho wife came on board. I guess he spotted her or found out somehow that she was on the ship and knew he had to hide. When I went to his cabin it was clear he'd not slept in the bed. Then I made things worse for him by circulating his picture to all the food outlets. He couldn't even buy food, so he found a way to steal it. He's been sleeping in the cleaning rooms too."

"But not this one?" Lady Mary sought to confirm.

"He hits a different room every time. My guess is that he feels bad about taking their food and doesn't want to do it to the same person twice. That or he believes he is less likely to get caught if he keeps moving about. Either way, he is not here, so we will try a different deck."

On the way I explained why the cleaners don't take their lunch in one of the mess rooms reserved for the crew. There are fresh meals available through the day to meet the needs of constantly changing watches – a ship is a twenty-four-hour a day operation.

"They finish their work when they finish their work. Each of them has a set number of cabins to clean and their practice is to eat on the go. That way they finish quicker and get more leisure time. I'm led to believe they all operate the same way."

"Huh. I never knew that," said Barbie.

On deck eleven, in another cleaning storeroom, I knew we had found someone who did not want to be found the moment I opened the door. There was an unquantifiable stillness to the air that one only gets when a person or animal is holding their breath and pretending they don't exist.

"Dale?" I called my voice friendly. "Dale, I'm here to rescue you from your wife."

No response came.

"I know what she is, Dale. I know you are trying to escape her, and I know she brought two of her goons along to help find you. You don't have to hide anymore. I have lots of armed security officers with me. They can protect you."

There was no sound from within, no sense that my words were reaching anyone, but hiding spaces abounded, even for a man of Dale's size.

When a voice echoed out of the gloom, it still caught me by surprise.

"Is she in custody?"

"Not yet."

"Then you can't protect me. You don't know her. I went to the police and they just laughed at me. I've tried to get away before, but she always finds me. When I told my parents I thought they were going to disown me. My father said I had to stand up to her. She broke my arm and dislocated my shoulder when I tried. Please, just shut the door and leave me in here."

He sounded broken.

My voice soft and caring, I said, "It is going to be different this time, Dale. She is going to go to jail, but I need your help to achieve that. You can trust me, Dale. I am on your side."

He didn't reply, so I waited in silence to give him time. The way I saw it, he knew he couldn't continue to hide in a storeroom living on other people's lunches and he couldn't hide from his wife forever. His only way out was to beat her, and I was offering a way to do it.

More than a minute passed before he moved, the sound of a foot shuffling a few inches enough to make Barbie smile with relief. I felt it too. Our work isn't about helping people, not directly, though there are generally those who benefit when we take down a criminal. Today though, today we were going to make a difference for Dale Morris.

From the shadows at the back of the storeroom, the tall, muscular form of Stephanie's husband emerged. His strides were faltering, not confident, his posture shrunken and his head down as though he could hide from the world if he just concentrated hard enough on being invisible.

I held out my hand, offering it for him to take. Not so he could shake it in greeting, but so I could lead him to safety.

Timidly, he asked, "You have a plan?"

Bedlam

I hadn't called Stephanie earlier. I was about to when people started asking me questions and I perceived a better strategy. Now that Dale was with us, we could draw Stephanie into a trap. There was some risk, I'll not deny it, but the pros massively outweighed the cons.

We knew she had her phone because she sent a text to Edgar to ask where he and Mason were. She used colourful language to demand they stop messing about, remove their thumbs from somewhere I thought it improbable they would put them, and get on with the task she set them. She followed it with a threat to cut off parts of their anatomy I believed they would sorely miss if they allowed her husband to evade them.

Armed with knowledge and a plan, I tried, yet again, to call Stephanie. As before she ignored my attempt to speak with her. Anticipating that she would, I already had a text message in my head.

Fingers flashing across my phone, I wrote, '*Stephanie, we have located him! He's just been spotted on deck seven. I'm sure this must all be terrifying for you, and I get why you are ducking my calls, but I have security officers closing in on him as I type.*' I left it at that and waited.

She would either take the bait or she would not.

More than a minute passed before a text pinged back. '*Oh, my goodness, Patricia. I cannot tell you how much this means to me. I was so scared sitting in the sickbay all by myself. When the prime minister left and took the armed guards with him, I just couldn't stay there. I've been hiding in a toilet cubicle ever since. Please let me know when you have him in custody. I won't feel safe until then.*'

Her charade was convincing, but she spoiled it a moment later, when she sent a second message.

'*Where was he spotted on deck seven?*'

I felt my mouth curl into a smile to challenge the Cheshire Cat. *Gotcha.*

I fired off a swift reply and pocketed my phone.

Barbie did not share my jubilation. "Patty, are you sure about this?" Stephanie wanted to kill her husband. She'd said as much herself, only she voiced it from the other direction as if she were the one trying to escape. That she might succeed was Barbie's big concern, and she wasn't alone. If I asked permission for what I proposed to do, it would be firmly denied. For that reason alone, I opted to beg for forgiveness afterwards.

I laughed. "Sure about it? Heck no. I'm not the one taking all the risk, though." I turned to the man who was. "Ready?"

Whether he was or not no longer mattered because it was go time. We were already in place and I had Commander Jandl and three dozen of his guards positioned strategically around the ship on decks seven and eight. They were covering stairwells and elevators, so Dale wouldn't be able to double back and escape. That's what I wanted Stephanie to see. I needed her to believe we were still hounding her husband. I wanted her to believe she could find him first, and move in.

She would try to kill him; of that I was certain. What weapon she might employ I could not guess, though a knife or stabbing implement of some kind seemed most likely. To catch her in the act, my team and more were sewn through the crowd of passengers in their every-day clothes.

Their watchful eyes would identify her long before she moved in and possession of the weapon would show enough intent to get her locked up. Not forever, but with additional evidence from Dale, coupled with the fact that she followed him to the ship and brought along Mason and Edgar, who I believed would give evidence against her, there would be enough for Dale to get clear once and for all.

We gave Stephanie enough time to get from wherever she might have been to deck seven, then sent our bait on his route. He had his hood up to hide his face, and walked with his shoulders folded down and in – the appearance of a man trying to hide despite being inches taller than the average person. He stood out like a giraffe at a zebra party, but that was kind of the point.

I wanted him to be visible.

He had a pack on his back and a small blue suitcase in his left hand. In his right he gripped his passport tightly.

Deck seven is mostly taken up by cabins, but to give the impression of size and opulence, and to provide the space required to carry out passport and security checks the main entrance/exit is a wide space made double height by eating up some room from deck eight. Passengers must be booked in an out, much the same as staying in a hotel, so to avoid congestion they are given arrival and departure times. Even so, the area was filled with people excited to get off the ship. Hawaii and all its wonders beckoned.

PRIME SHOT

Skirting the outer edge and finding spots where I could be out of sight yet keep watch, I spotted Deepa through the crowd. Being a gym instructor, Barbie wasn't part of the operation, but she refused to be left behind and was at Deepa's side. The pair of them were chatting amiably, but their excitement was an act. Their eyes roved the crowd, searching for Stephanie.

I checked the bait again. He lumbered onward, making his way slowly to the desk where he would be checked off and bade a fond farewell.

A cry of alarm from my left pulled my attention and caused my pulse to race. Someone was shouting about being cut and that they were bleeding. Across the room, Commander Jandl caught my eye. I shook my head and he stayed in place.

My heart beat a little quicker. Was this it? The injured woman continued to wail about the blood running down her arm. She would be dealt with soon enough, but was she an unwitting distraction?

An instant later, and twenty yards from where a crowd had gathered around the injured woman, multiple squeals of fright erupted. They were followed by a loud hiss and the unmistakable whoosh of a firework zipping across the room.

People scattered, bolting outward from the source of the firework only to meet more coming the other way when it crashed into a bulkhead on the far side of the room. There it exploded in a blinding flash of light and I realised I was seeing a flare, not a firework. The phosphorous dropped to the deck where it immediately set fire to a display stand showing the many activities available on board.

Screams and cries of panic filled the air. Leaving my spot against the wall, I thrust myself into the crowd. Swallowed immediately by the crowd, I had to fight to cross the room. Crew battled to get to the fire, but it was on the other side of a stampede. Passengers of all ages surged away from the flames, the pace too fast for some of the more elderly or frail. Yet more cries arose as some fell and risked being trampled.

The entire area had gone from the contained excitement of passengers looking forward to the day ahead to utter bedlam in the space of a few seconds. I held no doubt Stephanie was behind it, which was why I fought to reach Dale.

From my radio came a stark warning. "We've got a man down! This Bulwark. Stokes has been stabbed and his sidearm is missing! Over."

My breath caught. It had to be Stephanie and now she was armed. My plan failed to consider that she might steal a gun.

"I saw her!" shouted Deepa, her voice carrying across the radio airwaves.

Dale twisted left and right. Frozen to the spot, he couldn't decide which way to go, but through the crowd I saw Stephanie stalking him. She was bent at the waist, her knees flexed to keep her body low and out of sight. I couldn't track her; she was there one moment and gone the next.

Getting my elbows to work, I forced my way through the sea of people. To my left fire extinguishers were being deployed. The noise competing with the cacophony of shouts from both passengers and crew. Smoke drifted on the air, but we were in no great danger. The fire wouldn't take hold, but my focus was on Dale. He wouldn't see his wife until she struck.

Shouting into my radio, I bellowed, "She's about to attack him!"

Three shots rang out in quick succession. The already spooked crowd ducked as one, yet more shouts of terror competing with the echoing sound of gunfire.

Someone's suitcase struck my right knee, knocking my leg out from under me. I stumbled but did not fall. Yet when I recovered to my full height Dale was nowhere to be seen.

"Does anyone have eyes on the target?" I shouted only for my voice to be lost in the din of trampling feet and terrified shouts. Cursing myself, I tried again, this time using my radio.

I got negatives from a dozen sources, all of whom were converging on Dale's last location. Where the heck was he?

The answer came a moment later when I broached the back edge of the crowd. They were still dispersing, trying to get out of the entranceway and back into the ship's superstructure. That created a gap and in the centre of it lay Dale, flat on his front, smoke rising from three holes in his back.

Shot in the Back

I stared in mute horror. To my right, from the corner of my eye, I saw Stephanie tackle one of the ship's security guards. He'd drawn his weapon and was pointing it in her direction, but in the split second he had to take the shot, he'd questioned whether it was right to do so, and lost the opportunity.

She ripped the weapon from his hands and might have turned it on him, had she not then been tackled to the ground by Commander Jandl himself. More officers rushed in to assist as the diminutive brunette fought like a hellcat.

Her gun discharged into the air as she went down to the deck, but she was far from done. Two of the guards trapped her right hand, whacking it against the deck to jar the gun free.

Despite all that was happening just a few yards away, I couldn't take my eyes off the body. My right foot started to move. I wanted to go to him, but my legs betrayed me and stopped before I'd even taken the first step. I'd always known this was a possibility, but I never truly believed she'd get within striking distance.

Deepa and Barbie rushed past me. They'd fought their way through the panicked crowd, and now they were in the clear they ran to Dale's side, dropping to their knees to check on him.

All around me, it was utter mayhem. Passengers were still attempting to leave the area. Crew were still trying to extinguish the fire. Injured passengers drew the attention of the available crew, and all the while Stephanie continued to fight with the guards.

Some were hurt, their white uniforms stained red with blood, but with a bark of triumph and a cry of frustrated rage from Stephanie, I heard cuffs ratchet home. Yet I still couldn't take my eyes off the body.

Only when Barbie looked my way did I finally turn my attention to the perpetrator—the killer in our midst.

Hauled from the deck by her shoulders, I saw blood coming from a cut in Stephanie's bottom lip and more from a wound inside her hairline. Her hands were restrained behind her back, she had been disarmed, and there was no chance she would escape justice. Not with so many witnesses, yet a smile pulled at the corners of her mouth.

"Well, well, well. I guess I have to congratulate you. I was beginning to think all the hype about you was in error, but you finally figured it out."

"I had some help, but yes, I got there in the end."

She smirked and cast her eyes to the body lying prone on the deck behind me. "A bit late though, wouldn't you say? I told him what would happen if he ever tried to leave me again. Honestly, I don't see how I can be held accountable. He caused this, not me."

"You could have just let him get on with his life while you got on with yours."

She shook her head and gave a little tinkle of laughter. "And go back on my word? In the navy we used words like honour, courage, family. He didn't understand any of that and it's clear you don't either. Honestly though, I'm disappointed it's all over so quickly. I didn't want to do it like this. I'd decided to let him leave the ship. I wanted him to think he'd got away and was safe. He would have found somewhere to go and a job would have come along. My plan was to wait until he'd settled into life and found a girlfriend. Then I could surprise them in bed together." She giggled in a slightly deranged way. "That would have been fun. I would gut them both. Her first, of course, just so he would know what was coming. Till death do us part, Patricia. He said it and so did I. One of us meant it and if the other didn't … well, that's why this was necessary. To make sure he understands that vows are vows."

I raised my eyebrows and looked at Commander Jandl. "You got all that?"

"I did." He took a phone from his pocket, tapped an app and pressed play. Stephanie's confession filled the silence.

She shrugged. "Whatever. It was totally worth it."

I held up an index finger, begging she give me a moment. Rotating to face Deepa and Barbie where they still crouched over the body, I asked, "How's he doing?"

Deepa said, "Let's check," and tapped Dale's shoulder.

Both women moved back a foot, giving the body room and I made sure to be looking Stephanie's way when the corpse performed a press up and got to its feet.

Stephanie's face made me wish I was holding a camera. From shock to misunderstanding and onward to rage, the full gamut of emotions battled for superiority. They settled on outright disbelief when Dale then lifted his head and removed the hood of his top to reveal Lieutenant Schneider's face.

Stephanie blurted, "But …"

Schneider unzipped the top, pulled off his t-shirt and proceeded to unstrap the bulky Kevlar vest he wore beneath. The idea to switch him out with Stephanie's husband came only when I finally met Dale. Schneider is shorter and not as wide, but the difference is negligible and can only be seen when they are standing next to each other. A wig to change Schneider's hair plus Dale's clothes to complete the transformation and his own wife, quite literally, couldn't tell the difference.

"Where is Dale?" Stephanie demanded, her words laced with incandescent rage.

I gave Commander Jandl a nod and turned away. "Goodbye, Stephanie."

She continued to scream blue murder and vengeance until her voice faded into the distance.

The fire was out, the drama was over, but there were still tasks to which I had to attend before I could hope to go ashore.

First on the list was Prime Minister Filipovic.

The Press Conference

Once things started to settle down, I was able to confirm the Molovian Prime Minister was among the first to leave the ship. He'd missed all the drama, but that was good. I didn't want anything to distract him from the press conference he planned to give on the quayside.

Commander Jandl wanted my team to handle Stephanie. She needed to be processed along with Mason and Edgar before being handed over to the Honolulu PD. But that wouldn't happen until after the bulk of passengers had disembarked – no need to air our laundry in public and all that. Any more than is necessary, anyway. That gave us time, which was good because I needed them for what was coming next. I needed Commander Jandl too, and a bunch of his officers. He understood why when I outlined my plan.

Also with me were Barbie and Lady Mary who had wisely elected to avail herself of the upper deck bar while we baited Stephanie with Lieutenant Schneider. There, and accompanied by Lieutenant Commander Martin Baker and a duo of the ship's security guards, she kept Dale company and educated him in the ways of gin.

She certainly seemed more relaxed when she returned, so if he kept up with her I imagined he was halfway to hammered.

Mopping things up and getting onto the quayside took longer than anticipated, and I missed the start of the PM's speech. He'd called it a press conference, but he was the only one talking.

His wife stood behind and to his right. In his shadow as always.

"Don't mind me," said Lady Mary as we approached him. "You lot just crack on. I'll catch up with you shortly."

I looked around to question what she meant only to find her wandering away. It looked as though she was heading for one of the market sellers the docks always attract. Had it really been that long since her last drink?

Radovan Filipovic was back in a suit, his politician's smile plastered firmly in place unless he needed to make a serious point. His words became clearer as we drew near to the low stage on which he was standing. The press corps gathered to his front were filled with those who'd followed him all over the ship, but they made up only half the number by rough calculation. The rest displayed banners from news channels and agencies from around the world. I picked out BBC and CNN instantly.

"... upon my return to Molovia, I will instigate an investigation into the criminal acts perpetrated on behalf of my rival candidate, Lisik Ramovich. His negative campaigning, the falsehoods he told, and most recently the attempts upon my life will see him fail in his bid to become my beloved Molovia's next prime minister. Instead, I believe the people will find him guilty of my attempted murder and he will spend much of the rest of his life in jail."

My approach was spotted by a cameraman's assistant about twenty yards from the stage. I saw him tap the man with a camera and stand on tiptoes to whisper in his ear. He kept the camera on its target while he risked a peek.

I lifted my left hand to give him a pinky wave and a cheeky grin.

The camera was on me in a heartbeat and others soon followed suit as the message rippled down the line.

"Now?" asked Barbie.

"Yes. Make the call." I didn't need to look to know she had her phone in her hand.

Prime Minister Filipovic didn't notice at first, but I saw him glance my way when he did. Ever the professional, he kept right on talking as though nothing was happening.

With my team at my back, I reached the edge of the stage where the prime minister's bodyguard held out a hand to stop me.

"One chance," I warned. "Step aside or you go straight to the brig." Actually, he was going to the brig whether he stepped aside or not, but I didn't want to make a scene just yet.

Grigore made a scoffing noise. "We're not on the ship anymore, lady."

Dismissing him as unimportant, I said, "Take him," and continued onward to mount the stage. He attempted to grab me as I slipped by, but was yanked off his feet by Deepa, Schneider, Sam, and Molly.

I continued across the stage without so much as a glance over my shoulder. I didn't need to see to know they were wrestling Grigore to the ground.

The phalanx of press all turned their attention away from the PM, but they couldn't decide if they wanted to see the PM's bodyguard getting arrested, or whether the infamous Patricia Fisher was about to do something newsworthy.

Well, I was, and for once I was glad the press could recognise me.

There was no option to continue to ignore me, so the prime minister made the best of it.

"Ladies and gentlemen, we have a special guest with us today. Please welcome to the stage, Patricia Fisher." He held out an arm to welcome me in, but I stopped well out of his reach. Adapting, he turned back to the cameras. "Mrs Fisher and I worked hand in hand in a bid to catch the assassin. I imagine she is here now with yet another update." He looked at me with a hopeful expression. "Have you been able to catch the man who tried to kill me, Mrs Fisher?"

He thought the question was a trap. He believed I was just as in the dark as ever and hoped to expose my failure.

"Yes, thank you, Radovan." I made a point of using his first name. He wasn't my prime minister. "The press just witnessed me arresting him."

Momentarily lost for words, Radovan stuttered a little when he managed to respond.

"Surely you are confused, Mrs Fisher. Your team appear to have arrested my bodyguard."

"That's correct. Shortly, they will arrest the fake reporters you brought on board to chronicle the equally fake attempted assassinations you arranged."

There were nervous glances passing between the reporters I'd come to recognise as his. They'd followed him everywhere he went for the last three days and captured his finest moments to create a hero of his nation.

At my nod, Commander Jandl double-timed a squad of officers across the quayside. In their splendid white uniforms they evoked the elegance of the Aurelia. They spread out behind the line of press, trapping them against the ship.

Radovan moved away from the microphone, coming to me when I didn't go to him.

"What is this nonsense, Mrs Fisher? None of what you say is true and you have no evidence. Back away or I will make a laughingstock of you. I am the hero of Molovia. Its leader. Its champion. You are just some old woman on a cruise ship. Well, you might have a modicum of power there, but we are no longer on your ship, are we?"

I smiled. His bodyguard made the same mistake.

"Actually, we are."

"Are what?"

"Still on the ship. In a technical sense, that is. You see, until you pass through those gates over there," I pointed to the official border for Hawaii some fifty yards away, "you are still on the quayside and that means maritime law still applies."

"No, it doesn't," he scoffed in amusement. Then, seeing the seriousness on my face and all those around me, he asked, "Does it?"

My smile broadened and I walked around him to get to the microphone.

"Hello, everyone. My name is Patricia Fisher ..."

"This is my press conference!" Radovan spat, racing to wrestle the microphone from me. He got about halfway before Molly's foot tripped him and he sprawled across the stage, the wind rushing from his lungs in a giant 'Oooff'.

I had glanced down at him, and needed a moment to stifle my amused expression before facing the cameras once more.

"Where was I? Oh, yes. The assassination attempts on the prime minister where carefully staged misses intended to divert attention away from his recently exposed affair with Bianca Vladinova."

"That's a lie," Radovan groaned from the stage floor.

"He also hoped to accuse his opponent of the crimes and turn the tide of opinion in his favour with some carefully timed and cleverly worded soundbites. Indeed, I believe his strategies were working, but he brought danger to the passengers of the Aurelia, injured at least one person, and caused damage to the ship in his bid to trick Molovia into trusting him."

Radovan clambered awkwardly to his feet with Schneider and Deepa poised to grab him. They looked surprised when I shook my head, but I wanted to finish this properly.

Striding confidently toward the microphone, Radovan snapped, "I've had enough of this rubbish. You will be hearing from my lawyers."

I stepped out of his way, freeing the microphone for his use with a parting comment, "And I imagine you will be hearing from your wife's." I backed away and turned to address her. "Mrs Filipovic, I have someone who would like to speak with you."

Throughout his speech and the subsequent interruptions, the prime minister's wife hadn't moved or said a word, but she had a key part to play and it was time to involve her.

The prime minister had one hand on the microphone stand and his mouth open, but whatever salvo he planned to launch died in his mouth.

"Wait, what are you doing? Who wants to talk to my wife?"

I waved for Barbie to come forward. Since we arrived at the side of the stage, Barbie had been chatting on her phone.

She said, "I'll hand you over now."

Radovan repeated his demand.

"Oh, it's Bianca Vladinova," I replied, as though the name of the woman he denied having an affair with was of no consequence.

His wife's eyes almost popped out on stalks and she grabbed for the phone. In his haste to stop her, Radovan barrelled into me. I lost my footing, but for once didn't fall flat on my face because Deepa was there to catch me.

Barbie blocked the prime minister's path and handed the phone to his wife while glaring down at the short man.

"Don't answer that!" Radovan barked at his wife. "I order you to hang up."

His wife's look of incredulity doubled, and she said, "This is she," in clear tones everyone could hear.

"No! You must hang up now! Don't listen to any of that woman's lies!"

"Oh, he did, did he? Well, yes, he's always liked it when I did that. What? Well, if you think I should." She moved the phone away from her face and covered it with her other hand. "If you admit the truth, it will stay with me. I will divorce you quietly after the election. You can have your throne, but I am taking the house in the country and your collection of vintage cars."

"But that's my family home! You can't have it," he hissed, keeping his voice quiet so the press wouldn't hear.

She quirked her elegant eyebrows and matched his whisper. "I tolerated you being a boorish politician all these years. I even put up with your tiny wiener, but cheating on me with a younger woman, that I will not stand. Take your pick, Radovan. Your career or your ancestral home. Either way, I'm no longer part of the package, so choose which one you want to lose."

His hands flexed into impotent fists. He was beaten and he knew it.

He swore under his breath and spat, "You can have the house. And the cars."

"So you admit the affair?" his wife pushed him to say it.

"Yes," he grunted. Raising his focus from his shoes to glare into his wife's eyes, he whispered a snarl, "What did you expect? You really thought a man of my status would continue to put up with your sagging backside? I can have any woman I want."

"I wouldn't be too sure about that," said Barbie.

Ignoring her, he added, "Once I win the election, women will flock to my bed. Just you wait and see. There's probably a line of them waiting for me right now. I'll have replaced you by sunset."

I tapped him on the shoulder and when he looked my way I used my head to indicate that he should look up.

In pseudo slow motion, he angled his head back to spot the boom above his head. When he stepped away from the microphone, I had signalled to the press that they should close in behind us. The real press that is, not Radovan's team of flunkies. They had recorded everything and now his election chances really were over.

"Are we done?" called Lady Mary.

Barbie took the phone back from Radovan's wife and handed it to the prime minister. "Someone wants to talk to you."

Putting it to his ear, he whined, "Why did you do that to me? I thought we had a connection."

Lady Mary said, "I'm sure you did."

Confused, Radovan took the phone away from his ear to find all those around him laughing.

"What's going on? Where's Bianca? Who am I talking to now?"

I backed away and gestured that everyone else should distance themselves, too. "The same person your wife was talking to the whole time. Lady Mary Bostihill-Swank. She advised your wife to play along and that she could finally get the truth about your affair with little more than a hastily concocted ruse. You see, I don't have the evidence I need to prove Grigore fired the arrow and dropped the dumbbell, but viewed from a certain angle, he looks quite a bit like Dale Morris. That's Stephanie Morris's husband," I explained before he could ask. "Weirdly, he didn't show up on the list of potential suspects for the assassin, so I never looked at him until I realised he'd slipped an Airtag into my handbag. Then you used the word 'staged' when I suggested there wasn't really an assassin on the ship. I've got some work to do to make sure the case against you is sound, but I'll get there now that I know what to look for. That's why I had to let you sabotage yourself over the affair you had. I'm sure it wasn't the only one, but you faked the attempts on your life just to get ahead of it. Now the world knows, and your country can finally vote for someone who will work for them."

He saw how he'd been tricked. Saw his election slipping away along with any hope of a career anywhere in politics. The worst of it was yet to hit him because I was going to throw not just the book but the entire library at him. He arranged to have an arrow fired on board the ship I love. He could have killed someone with the dumbbell and the bullet that winged him could have hit anyone. His bodyguard perpetrated the crimes, but not for his own benefit. Grigore would turn and lay everything at his boss's door. Of that I had little doubt.

A tomato hit Radovan in the head.

"Boooooo!" shouted Lady Mary and threw another.

I had asked her to play the part of Bianca Vladinova because she has just the right measure of mature indignation when it comes to philandering men. I hadn't expected her to buy crates of tomatoes though. That was clearly why she had peeled off toward the market stalls.

Her next boo and next tomato were joined by others as the crowd turned against the self-proclaimed hero of Molovia.

Arms raised to protest, he tried to convince the press and everyone present that he was being falsely accused and would clear his name once he'd had time to speak with his advisors. His words fell on deaf ears as the tomatoes came thick and fast.

Only once they ran out of ammunition did I ask Deepa and Molly to take the prime minister into custody.

Dinner

A few hours later, I met Alistair for a late dinner in a little place he knew. His years of circling the globe have given him an almost encyclopaedic knowledge when it comes to hidden gems in remote locations. When he says he has somewhere he wants to take me, I never question it.

A candle flickered on the table to my right. Stuffed into an old chianti bottle, dribbles of wax from a hundred previous candles coated the sides.

He had my hand in his and for what was possibly the first time since we first kissed, I felt nervous. There were butterflies in my stomach because he had a look about him that made me think he was going to ask me a question. A very particular question that tends to come with a ring attached.

And I didn't know how I would answer. I was in love with him, that was not in question, but after thirty years married to Charlie, and with the ink on our divorce still drying, did I really want to get married again?

Sensing he was about to speak, and desperate to postpone my need to give a response if he did pop 'the question', I got in first.

"We found enough evidence to put the squeeze on Grigore Volantin. He visited the top deck gym sixty-three minutes before the incident with the dumbbell. The camera shows how much heavier his gym bag is on the way out."

"He gave up his boss?"

"He sure did, but Filipovic didn't have a lot of wiggle room. He lied about sending his bodyguard to the spa. That's where he said he was when the first assassination attempt took place. The moment we pushed Grigore to account for his whereabouts at specific times, he knew the game was up. But the real breakthrough came when Deepa and I sat down with his wife."

Alistair jinked an eyebrow. "A woman scorned?"

"Pretty much. She knew he was up to something with the press and constantly sending his bodyguard away. The poor woman admitted to sticking her head in the sand and that it had been there for years. It's out now though. She gave us bank statements showing payments to members of the press he brought on board with him. They are real reporters, by the way, but ones with either no career or aspirations of greatness as part of the prime minister's press team. He'd offered positions and made all manner of promises to them."

"Let me guess, they also turned on him."

I nodded. "They sure did."

"And what of Stephanie Morris?"

I picked up my wineglass and took a sip. I had been ready to help that woman and it stung to know it was all a lie. A really cruel, twisted lie contrived to pull at my heartstrings.

"She stabbed a member of the crew and stole his sidearm. That's being added to the list of offences. Dale's attempted murder takes precedence, though, so she was handed to the Honolulu PD. They have to figure out how to handle the mess. She is an Australian citizen, but she attempted to murder an American. Ordinarily, they would be able to charge her, but the crime occurred on the ship which is outside of their jurisdiction. Regardless, she is in custody and will stay there until a decision is made about where she will stand trial and her longer-term incarceration."

"And her bounty hunters?"

"They gave her up in a heartbeat. In separate statements to my team, they each confirmed she brought them on board to find and catch her husband. They didn't know she planned to kill him. Or so they claim. However, they attacked and injured a member of the crew." My mind flicked to an image of Jermaine with his head bandaged. "I would like to see them locked up, but Stephanie is the bigger fish. They are also with the Honolulu PD, but I expect to see them walk with a slap on the wrist if they give evidence against her." Wistfully, I added, "It's out of my hands now."

"And Dale?" Alistair was asking all the right questions, but I couldn't shift the feeling that he was poised to steer the conversation in a different direction.

"Dale was relieved to see his wife taken away in cuffs, but also saddened by it. He thought he was escaping and that he'd covered his tracks so she wouldn't even know he had gone, let alone where he was, but he saw her getting on the ship. He'd been to his cabin and was looking over the side of the ship when she arrived with Mason and Edgar. Knowing he couldn't go back to his cabin, he went into hiding."

"He was hiding for the whole passage?"

"And living on scraps of food he found, plus a few stolen lunches. There must have been a time when they were in love. It's hard for me to imagine how their relationship became so toxic. He didn't want to talk about it, and he knew he would be required to give detailed statements to the police."

"He'll have no choice if he wants her to be convicted."

I sat in silence for a moment, my thought broken when Alistair spoke again.

"You seem distant, my love."

I gave a one shoulder shrug. "I was chasing the wrong person right until the very end. There was a point when I would have cheered if someone accidentally shot Dale. This could have ended so differently."

"But it didn't, darling. You got the right people in the end."

"In the end," I agreed. Was I being tough on myself? Was it a bad thing if I was? There would be more cases to solve on board the Aurelia. My record for catching the bad people was almost perfect, but even now I had one outstanding case: the necklace from Bingley's. Just how had that thing ended up on the ship?

Heist

Justin clapped his hands together. "Ready?"

The Honolulu branch of the First Hawaiian Bank on South Beretania Street was about to suffer its first ever raid. Not that Justin intended to steal anything. The raid was to act as a diversion, pulling the police across the city, so they were busy when he hit the real target: a stockbroker agency.

Research was the key to Justin's success. That and diversity. Most thieves pick a speciality and stick with it. They rob banks or they steal art and they stay in their lane because building up the contacts to shift the stolen goods is harder than pulling off the crime itself.

Justin varied his targets as much as his methods and only used a crew once if he could help it. To pull each team together, he employed a network of contacts via the dark web and never used his own name.

Tonight's target was a hundred million dollars in bearer bonds. His cut was to be a paltry ten percent, which was another reason why he had no difficulty recruiting help. He didn't need the money. For him this was just sport, so his five-person team were all getting twenty percent of the remaining ninety million dollars.

Confident to an extreme degree, Justin counted down with his fingers and pointed to the demolition expert who pressed a button on his laptop. Nothing happened for more than a second, then a hole the size of a door blew outward from the western face of the bank and a warbling alarm filled the air.

The rest would be easy enough. In fact, to Justin's mind, the hardest part was going to be leaving Patricia a clue she would see but not understand. Not yet.

Befriending her went better than he could have expected. She thought of him as a sweet old man. A fatherly or even grandfatherly figure given the four decades between them. And she was right, he was all of those things.

He was also the world's greatest thief and had just about enough life and energy in him to prove it one last time.

The End

Book 11 is waiting for you. Scan the QR code with your phone to find your copy of Island Life.

Author's Notes:

Hello, Dear Reader,

Thank you for reading all the way to the end of the story and beyond. When I first started writing these little author's notes at the back of my books, it was to explain some of the British terminology I believed might cause confusion to people not from these islands.

However, it felt very dry, so I expanded my scope to include what was happening in the world – the books written in 2020 outline the pandemic and I wonder if my notes might be read a century from now with more interest in them than the content of the book.

I often include a note or two about my own life, so to that end I can tell you it is nearing Christmas. The weather is cool but still above freezing, but snow or temperatures below zero are rare here. Winter tends to be a boring grey drizzle rather than the flurry of glorious white flakes all the children yearn for.

I take extra time out of my day to be with the children in the build up to the big day. They are giddy with excitement anyway, so it feels right to make hot chocolates to revive chilly cheeks after the walk home from school. And what better way to drink them than on the sofa with a seasonal movie?

Despite painting that rosy, cosy picture this book took me almost two months to complete. I was scheduled to write 'The End' before the children broke up from school, but concern about our four-year-old daughter's eyesight led us to a specialist hospital department who instantly admitted her.

Over the course of a few weeks, she went from what we perceived to be perfect eyesight to effectively blind and no one can tell us why or whether it will ever come back. They have ruled out all the worst things and performed tests on her head that show her eyes function perfectly. Somewhere between the back of her eye and her brain, the signal is going awry.

Why am I telling you this? For no other reason than I have been sharing snippets from my life and adventures since I started writing. I announced the pregnancy in a book. I announced Hermione's birth in a book. When I have better news about her health, I will share that too.

In this story Patricia uses Royal Tonbridge Wells as a code to discuss the royal wedding. The town had other names across the centuries, but was frequented by the royal family so often that King Edward VII granted the town the 'Royal' prefix in 1909. There are only two other towns in England to have earned that honour.

I touch briefly on the subject of night patrols. In the early part of my career as a soldier, I had the distinct displeasure of guarding the barracks. It was a task made necessary by terrorist organisations such as the IRA, who attacked multiple bases during my time in the military, killing and maiming whenever they could.

From first hand experience, I can assure you roving endlessly around a mile or so of perimeter fence is so boring one simply stops seeing it after a while. Much the same can be said for guarding a gate through which no one ever comes because the world is asleep at 0300hrs.

Nevertheless, I did my part and nothing ever exploded. For the security team on board the Aurelia, I believe night patrols will be no less monotonous.

I mention the Union Flag in this book. Many know it as the Union Jack, but that term only applies when it is raised on a Royal Navy vessel. Any other time it is a Union Flag. You might be surprised how many people in the United Kingdom don't know that.

Darius Kane crops up in this book, and if you are not aware, Patricia was recently in one of his adventures. Darius runs the Australian arm of Blue Moon Investigations, and if you have read Patricia's books you will know his boss, Tempest Michaels. Anyway, if you missed that story, you can find the cover and blurb below.

That's all for now. Thank you for reading. I have to get back to my daughter who now has chicken pox and thus cannot even attend the vital medical appointments she has this week.

Take care.

Steve Higgs

What's next for Patricia Fisher?

Moored among the tranquil islands off Thailand's coat, the Aurelia's passengers are completely unaware of the danger lurking just out of sight.

Patricia would happily remain oblivious, too, but that's not really how her life works. So when a couple report their teenage kids have gone missing, the ship's detective swings into action. Had she glimpsed the terror awaiting her, she might have thought twice.

There's a secret to uncover, the kind people will kill to protect, and she must expose it if there is any hope of rescuing the missing teenagers.

More alone than usual, running for her life, and short on plans, things don't look like they can get much worse. Which is when she sees the Aurelia sailing into the sunset without her on board.

Get ready for mystery and mayhem!

Did you Miss Patricia's Adventure in Australia?

Don't believe in magic? Boy are you in for a shock.

Convicted of a double homicide, the famous Wizard of Aus proves no cell can hold him, but his seemingly impossible prison break is more than a bid for freedom – he's got his sights set on vengeance – against the whole city.

Darius Kane thinks it's a job for the police and he's got his own work cut out trying to track down a secret underworld character more elusive than smoke. Known only as the Djinn, Darius must stop her if he wants to keep living.

However, when the wizard proves he can kill and vanish before the police can even react, can he really ignore the pleas for his involvement? Maybe, but when a new client enters the fray who might hold the key to identifying Darius's nemesis, there really is no choice but to take the case.

Alongside renowned English sleuth, Patricia Fisher, and her team, Darius must fight to find the connection between the wizard, the Djinn, and a criminal overlord and he'd better do it fast as the clock is ticking and the city is set to explode.

Free Books and More

Want to see what else I have written? Go to my website.

https://stevehiggsbooks.com/

Or sign up to my newsletter where you will get sneak peeks, exclusive giveaways, behind the scenes content, and more. Plus, you'll be notified of Fan Pricing events when they occur and get exclusive offers from other authors because all UF writers are automatically friends.

Copy the link into your web browser.

https://stevehiggsbooks.com/newsletter/

Prefer social media? Join my thriving Facebook community.

Want to join the inner circle where you can keep up to date with everything? This is a free group on Facebook where you can hang out with likeminded individuals and enjoy discussing my books. There is cake too (but only if you bring it).

https://www.facebook.com/groups/1151907108277718

Printed in Great Britain
by Amazon